She'd bought several pregnancy tests from this chemist without giving it a thought. Ellie panicked on regular occasions. But now that the test was for Alison she felt as if she knew half the shop, and was sure the girl serving was the daughter of one of her mum's friends—though hopefully she didn't recognise her.

They'd been careful, Alison told herself as she took her little parcel home.

But not quite careful enough, Alison realised as she stared at the little blue cross. And maybe it was coincidence, but as her mind drifted to Nick his must have drifted to her, because she felt the buzz of her phone.

Can I see you before I go?

Still sick, Alison replied.

I can come over—do you need anything?

She was tempted to text back *pram, cot, nappies*, but instead she wrapped up all the evidence in a paper bag, put that inside a carrier bag, and then into another one, and then put it in the outside bin before she texted him back the absolute truth.

I need space.

Dear Reader

Some people are naturally more cautious than others—that was certainly the case with my heroine, Alison. For her, it wasn't just a matter of nature, but nurture too—so I really felt for her when she looked up one morning into the gorgeous eyes of Nick and suddenly there it was: her chance to follow her heart and be just a little bit wild and have fun.

Given that I'm not particularly cautious, at times I just wanted to tell her to go for it—in fact, against Alison's better judgement, I *made* her go for it.

'I told you,' is still ringing in my ears.

Happy reading!

Carol x

HER
LITTLE SECRET

BY
CAROL MARINELLI

First published in Great Britain 2011
by Mills & Boon, an imprint of Harlequin (UK) Limited.
Large Print edition 2011
Harlequin (UK) Limited, Eton House,
18-24 Paradise Road, Richmond, Surrey TW9 1SR

ISBN: 978 0 263 21770 4

Harlequin (UK) policy is to use papers that are natural, renewable and recyclable products and made from wood grown in sustainable forests. The logging and manufacturing process conform to the legal environmental regulations of the country of origin.

Printed and bound in Great Britain
by CPI Antony Rowe, Chippenham, Wiltshire

Carol Marinelli recently filled in a form where she was asked for her job title, and was thrilled, after all these years, to be able to put down her answer as 'writer'. Then it asked what Carol did for relaxation. After chewing her pen for a moment Carol put down the truth—'writing'. The third question asked—'What are your hobbies?' Well, not wanting to look obsessed or, worse still, boring, she crossed the fingers on her free hand and answered 'swimming and tennis'. But, given that the chlorine in the pool does terrible things to her highlights, and the closest she's got to a tennis racket in the last couple of years is watching the Australian Open, I'm sure you can guess the real answer!

Carol also writes for
Mills & Boon® Modern™ Romance

Recent titles by the same author:

Medical™ Romance

RESCUED: PREGNANT CINDERELLA
(St Piran's Hospital)

Modern™ Romance

HIS CHRISTMAS VIRGIN
THE LAST KOLOVSKY PLAYBOY
(House of Kolovsky)

CHAPTER ONE

'AFTER you.'

Alison Carter gave brief thanks as someone stepped aside and she shuffled onto the bus, coffee in hand, and took a seat in her usual spot, halfway down, to the left of the bus and next to the window.

Morning was just peeking in and the sky was full of purples and oranges as the doors hissed closed and the bus made its slow way up the hill. Even though she'd bought a newspaper, till the bus turned the corner Alison did as she always did and stared out at the glorious view—to the energetic joggers on the foreshore, the walkers on the beach, the swimmers in the ocean and out beyond, to where the patient surfers bobbed quietly, waiting for the next good wave.

It was a slice of heaven.

A view that reminded Alison, because sometimes she needed reminding, that she lived in surely the most beautiful part of the world, that she had absolutely nothing to complain about. It was an internal pep talk that she delivered to herself quite often when the travel bug stung—yes, there were other beaches, other worlds to explore, but here was where she belonged and, if you had to be stuck somewhere, then Coogee was a very nice place to be…

Stuck.

Alison closed her eyes for just a second, leant her temple against the window and told herself to stop using that word.

Having recently read an article on positive thinking and the harm of negative self-talk and thoughts, she was resolutely reframing and rephrasing, but she was finding it to be an almost full-time job.

It was a very nice place to *be*, Alison told herself.

To just be!

As the bus took on its next load of passengers, then commenced its slow turn into the hilly street that would take them from Coogee to Eastern Beaches Hospital where she worked, Alison turned away to concentrate on her newspaper.

Then she saw him.

Craning his neck for a final glimpse of the beach too, it was, Alison was sure, the man who had let her on the bus before himself. The flash of blond hair and pale shirt that she'd glimpsed as she'd turned and briefly thanked him actually belonged to a man more beautiful than any she had ever seen and only then did she recall his English accent, and she was sure, quite sure, that the man she was looking at was *the* Nick Roberts.

Despite having been on days off from her job as an accident and emergency nurse, Alison had heard all about him from her friends and colleagues. Ellie had told her all about the gorgeous, *completely* gorgeous new locum registrar, who was filling in in Emergency while the senior registrar, Cort Mason, took some long overdue extended leave. Even Moira had sent her two texts worth of information about the nice surprise she'd found on her late shift one afternoon, warning her that he had to be seen to be believed.

Presuming that it was him, thanks to the hospital grapevine, and because nurses loved to gossip, Alison knew rather a lot about the handsome stranger on her bus. He had been travelling for six months and was doing a two-month stint in Sydney, getting some money together to spend on his prolonged journey home, first to New Zealand and then home to the UK via Asia, and, Ellie had said droolingly, while he was in Sydney, he was staying in Coogee.

It probably wasn't him, Alison told herself. Coogee was hardly the outback, there were loads of gorgeous men, loads of travellers, yet she was quite sure that it was him, because this man *had* to be seen to be believed.

Taller than most, he was sitting on a side seat, doing the crossword in the newspaper, and he kept forgetting to tuck his legs in, having to move them every time someone got on or got off. He had on dark grey, linen trousers and a paler grey shirt. And, yes, there were loads of Englishmen staying in Coogee—he could be anyone, but holidaymakers and travellers weren't usually on the two-minutes-past-six bus. It was, Alison knew, after nearly three years of taking this very route, a fairly regular lot she joined on the bus each morning.

Of course he caught her looking and he gave her a very nice smile, an open, possibly even flirting smile, and all it served to do was annoy Alison as she pulled her eyes away and back to her newspaper. In fact, she wanted to tell him that she'd been looking, not because he was drop dead gorgeous but because she thought she knew who he was.

And if she was right, then he'd be the last person she'd be interested in.

She'd heard all about him from her friends—the string of broken hearts he had left behind on his travels and daredevil attitude in his quest for adventure.

So, instead of thinking about him, Alison, as always, read her horoscope, which was too cryptic for such an early hour, so she turned, as she always did on a Friday, to the travel section, only the sting she so regularly felt became just a touch more inflamed as she read that airfares had come down dramatically. Even if it was too early for cryptic horoscopes the arithmetic was easy—her meticulous savings, combined with the money her father had left her, were enough for a tiny deposit on an even tinier flat or a round-the-world trip and a year or two spent following her heart.

Alison knew what her father would have chosen.

But she knew too what it would do to her mother.

She glanced up again to the man she thought was Nick Roberts. He had given up on his crossword and sat dozing now, and Alison stared, annoyed with a stranger who had been nothing but polite, jealous of a man she had never even met—because if this was Nick Roberts, then he was living her dream.

Maybe he felt her watching, because green eyes suddenly opened and met hers. He had caught her looking again and smiled. Embarrassed, Alison stood as her bus stop approached, and it was either be extremely rude or return his smile as she walked past.

'Morning,' Alison said, and then to show him she said morning and smiled at *everyone*, she said it to someone else who caught her eye as she moved down the bus.

And it *had* to be him because he was standing up too and this was the hospital bus stop and there certainly couldn't be two people as lovely as him working there.

They probably weren't, but Alison felt as if his eyes were on her as she walked through the car park and towards Emergency, and she was rather relieved when her friend and colleague Ellie caught up with her.

'Nice days off?' Ellie asked. 'Any luck with the flat-hunt?'

'None,' Alison admitted. 'Well, there was one flat that I could just about afford but it needs a kitchen.'

'You could live without a nice kitchen for a while,' Ellie pointed out.

'There's a hole in the side wall where the kitchen burnt down.' Alison managed a wry laugh as she recalled the viewing, the initial optimism as she'd walked through the small but liveable lounge, and then the sheer frustration as the renovator's delight that she'd thought she had found had turned out to be uninhabitable. 'It's impossible…' Alison carried on, but she'd lost her audience because Dr Long Legs had caught up, and Ellie, who never missed an opportunity to flirt, called over to him and he fell in step beside them.

'This is Alison. Alison, this is Nick,' Ellie

said, and none-too-discreetly gave her friend a nudge that said he was *the* Nick. 'He's with us for a couple of months.'

'Hi, Nick,' Alison said, and then to salvage herself, she gave him a smile. 'We met on the bus.'

'We did.'

'Anyone new tends to stand out—it's a pretty regular lot on the six a.m.,' Alison added, just to make it clear why she'd noticed him!

'Alison's flat-hunting,' Ellie said.

'Shoebox-hunting,' Alison corrected.

At twenty-four it was high past the time when she should have left home. Yes, most of her friends still lived at home and had no intention of leaving in a rush, but her friends didn't have Rose as a mother, who insisted on a text if she was going to be ten minutes late, and as for staying out for the night—well, for the stress it caused her mother it was easier just to go home.

Alison had moved out at eighteen to share a house with some other nursing students but at the end of her training, just as she'd been about to set off for a year of travel that her mother had pleaded she didn't take, her brother and father had died in an accident. Of course, she had moved straight back home, but though it had seemed right and necessary at the time, three years on Alison was beginning to wonder if her being there was actually hindering her mother from moving on. House-sharing no longer appealed and so the rather fruitless search for her own place had commenced.

'There are a couple of places I've seen that are nice and in my price range,' Alison sighed, 'but they're miles from the beach.'

'You're a nurse…' Ellie laughed. 'You can't afford bay views.'

'I don't need a view,' Alison grumbled, 'but walking distance to the beach at least…' She was being ridiculous, she knew, but she was so used to having the beach a five-minute walk away that it was going to be harder to give up than coffee.

'I'm on Alison's side.' Nick joined right in with the conversation. 'I'm flat-sitting for a couple I know while they're back in the UK.' He told her the location and Alison let out a low whistle because anything in that street was stunning. 'It's pretty spectacular. I've never been a beach person, but I'm walking there every morning or evening—and sitting on the balcony at night…'

'It's not just the view, though,' Alison said. They were walking through Emergency now. 'It's just…' She didn't really know how to explain it. It wasn't just the beach either—it was her walks on the cliffs, her coffee from the same kiosk in the morning, her cherry and ricotta strudel at her favourite café. She didn't want to leave it, her mother certainly didn't want her to leave either, but, unless she was going to live at home for ever, unless she was going to be home by midnight every night or constantly account for her movements, she wanted somewhere close enough to home but far enough to live her own life.

'I'm going to get a drink before…' He gave her a smile as they reached the female change rooms. 'I look forward to working with you.'

'Told you!' Ellie breathed as they closed the doors. 'I told you, didn't I?'

'You did,' Alison agreed, tying up her long brown hair and pulling on her lanyard. 'Have you got my stethoscope?'

'That's all that you've got to say?'

'Ellie, yes, you did tell me and, yes, for once you haven't exaggerated. He's completely stunning, but right now I need my stethoscope back.' She certainly didn't need to be dwelling on the gorgeous Nick Roberts who was there for just a few weeks and already had every woman completely under his spell.

'Here.' Ellie handed back the stethoscope she had yet again borrowed. 'Have a look at him on Facebook—there's one of him bungee-jumping and he's upside down and his T-shirt's round his neck…' Ellie grinned as Alison rolled her eyes. 'There's no harm in looking.'

Ellie raced off to the staffroom, ready to catch up on all the gossip, and for a moment Alison paused, catching sight of her reflection—brown hair, serious brown eyes, neat figure, smart navy pants and white top. Her image just screamed sensible. Too sensible by far for the likes of Nick. Yes, he was a fine specimen and all that, but he also knew it and Alison was determined not to give him the satisfaction of joining his rather large throng of admirers.

He was sitting in the staffroom as he had on the bus, with his long legs sprawled out, drinking a large mug of tea and leading the conversation as if he'd been there for years instead of one week, regaling them all with his exploits—the highlight a motorbike ride through the outback—which did nothing to impress Alison. In fact, the very thought made her shudder and prompted a question.

'How is that guy from last week?' Alison turned to Ellie. 'Did you follow him up?'

'What one?'

'Just as I went off last Sunday—the young guy on the motorbike?' And then she stopped, realising it sounded rude, perhaps a touch inappropriate given Nick's subject matter, though she hadn't meant it to. Nick had just reminded her to ask.

'We didn't have any ICU beds,' one of the other staff answered, 'so he was transferred.'

'Thanks,' Alison said, looking up at the clock,

and so did everyone else, all heading out for handover.

She really didn't want to like him.

He unsettled her for reasons she didn't want to examine and she hoped he was horrible to work with—arrogant, or dismissive with the patients. Unfortunately, he was lovely.

'I'm here for a good time, not a long time,' she heard him say to some young surfer who had cut his arm on the rocks. Nick was stitching as Alison came in to give the young man his tetanus shot. 'I want to cram in as much as I can while I'm here.'

'Come down in the morning,' surfer boy said. 'I'll give you some tips.'

'Didn't I just tell you to keep the wound clean and dry?' Nick admonished, and then grinned. 'I guess salt water's good for it, though. I'll look forward to it.'

'You're going surfing with him?' Alison blinked.

'He lives near me and who better to teach me than a local?' Nick said. 'Do you?'

'Do I what?'

'Surf.'

Alison rolled her eyes. 'Because I'm Australian?'

'No,' he said slowly, those green eyes meeting hers. 'Because you want to.' And she stood there for a moment, felt her cheeks darken, felt for just a moment as if he was looking at her, not staid, sensible Alison but the woman she had once been, or rather the woman she had almost become, the woman who was in there, hiding.

'If I wanted to, I would,' Alison replied, and somehow, despite the wobble in her soul, her voice was even. 'I've got a beach on my doorstep after all.'

'I guess,' Nick said, but she could almost hear his tongue in his cheek. 'I'll let you know what it's like.'

His assumption irritated her, perhaps more than it should have, but she wasn't going to dwell on it. She'd save a suitable come-back for later—perhaps this time tomorrow morning when she was stitching his forehead after his board hit him, Alison thought, taking the next patient card from the pile.

'Louise Haversham?' Alison called out to the waiting room, and when there was no answer she called the name again.

'Two minutes!' came the answer, a pretty blonde holding up her hand at Alison's interruption and carrying on her conversation on her phone, but perhaps realising that Alison was about to call the next name on the list she concluded her call and walked with Alison to a cubicle.

'How long have you had toothache for?' Alison asked, checking Louise's temperature and noting it on her card.

'Well, it's been niggling for a couple of weeks but it woke me up at four and I couldn't get back to sleep.'

'Have you seen your dentist?' Alison asked, and Louise shook her head.

'I've been too busy—I'm working two jobs.' She glanced up at the clock. 'How long will the doctor be? I'm supposed to be at work at nine.'

Then Alison had better hurry the doctor along!

'Who's next?' Nick asked cheerfully. 'A nice motorbike crash, perhaps?' He winked, just to show her he'd heard her in the staffroom.

'I'm saving the good stuff for later,' Alison said. 'I've got a toothache.'

'I'm sorry to hear it.'

She rolled her eyes at the very old joke, but it

did make her smile just a little bit and he *was* so easy to talk to, because somewhere between the work station and Cubicle Five she'd told him that she was going to the dentist herself next week. He opened the curtain where the very pretty blonde with a sore tooth that couldn't possibly wait till nine a.m. for a dentist was no longer chatting on her phone but cupping her jaw in her hand and looking an absolute picture of misery.

'Good morning.' He introduced himself and Louise introduced herself and managed, Alison noted, despite her agony, to perk up just a touch and give him a very brave smile.

'I'm so sorry.' She was far nicer to Nick than she had been to Alison. 'I just couldn't stand it any longer. I haven't slept all night…'

'Not at all. Dental pain's awful,' Nick said. Warning her he wasn't a dentist, he first had a feel of her jaw before he looked in her mouth, then long brown fingers examined her jaw again and felt around her neck. 'What was her temperature?' Nick asked, and Alison told him it was normal. 'There's no swelling. Still, I think we should give you something for the pain and a poultice for the tooth, but you really do need to see your dentist.' He turned round. 'Alison, do we have any oil of cloves?'

Right at the back of the treatment cupboard.

'Busy?' her friend Moira asked minutes later as she watched Alison curiously.

'Frantic!' She rolled her eyes to show that she wasn't in the least. 'I'm making an oil-of-cloves poultice,' Alison said, her own teeth slightly gritted.

'A what?' Moira frowned. 'What's that?'

'Some old English treatment. Actually, I remember my mum giving this to me once. I've never been asked for it.'

'Nick?' Moira checked and gave a little sigh.

'He asked me for some gentian violet yesterday.' She held up her palms to show the evidence. 'He dishes out the TLC, wish he'd dish some out in my direction!' Moira was Irish, just passing through Coogee too as she nursed and travelled her way around the world. She was fun and flirty and just…fun!

'Is he always so nice to everyone? It's like a social club in Section B.'

'Always,' Moira said cheerfully.

Returning to Cubicle Five, Alison wondered if he'd still be so nice when the place *was* frantic, but for now he was taking his time with his patient.

'Okay, Louise, I've given you a note for the dentist—you need to get that seen to this morning.'

Louise, once she'd bitten down on her cotton bud soaked in oil of cloves, managed to rally enough to tell him the name of the bar she worked at in the city, and that she was on at the weekend if he wanted to stop by for a drink on the house.

'I'm working…' Nick grinned '…but that's terribly kind of you.'

'He's worth getting toothache for,' Louise commented as he swept out and only the fresh scent of him lingered. They shared a little smile. 'If I suddenly come over all dizzy, will you call him back for me?'

'I'll get Amy, the other registrar.' Alison winked. 'She's good with dizzy females.'

'Shame.'

Nick changed the atmosphere of the place—he seemed delighted to be there, nothing was too trivial and nothing major unnerved him, as Alison found out when the husband of a swollen-ankle case suddenly complained of chest pain and started to pass out. Still Nick remained unruffled, breaking the gentleman's fall as Alison quickly wheeled out his wife, pressing the emergency bell and collecting the crash trolley.

By the time she returned, about twenty seconds later, the man had gone into full arrest and between them they had him clipped to the portable monitor, with Alison commencing cardiac massage even before help had arrived.

'Let's get him down to Resus.' Amy, the emergency registrar, called for a trolley, but Nick thought otherwise.

'Let's just keep going here.' It was a tiny override, or just a difference of opinion—nothing really—but when Amy, who easily took offence, simply nodded and they all just carried on working on the man on the cubicle floor, Alison realised the respect he had garnered in the short while he had been here.

Pads on, Nick shocked him, and before the

crash team had arrived, the poor man was back in sinus rhythm and starting to come round.

'It's okay, sir…' Nick's was absolutely the voice you wanted to come round to. He didn't talk down to the man and he didn't scare him as he lay there groaning. 'You're doing fine—your heart went into an irregular rhythm but it's beating normally now.' He smiled up to Amy. 'Okay, let's get him on a trolley and down to you guys. I'll go and speak with his wife.'

'What was he in for?' Amy asked.

'He's here with his wife, Doreen,' Nick explained. 'She's got an ankle injury.'

Having seen what was going on, Libby, the receptionist, had taken Doreen to an interview room and taken the husband's details from the shaken woman. After quickly writing his notes and checking the new patient's name, Nick walked down to the interview room with Alison.

He was very thorough, first checking her husband's details and assuming nothing—that Ernest was, in fact, her husband and finding out if she had contacted anyone. Then Nick got to the point, explaining that it would appear Ernest had had a heart attack.

'It probably doesn't feel it now, but your husband is an extremely lucky man—he could not have been in a better place when this happened.'

'Will he be okay?'

'We certainly hope so. He's conscious, the cardiologists will be running some tests now, but certainly the next twenty-four hours will be critical. I'm going to go and speak with my colleagues now and find out some more for you. I suggest you ring your son and get some family here to support you.' He stood and shook her hand. 'And I'll be back soon to take a good look at your ankle.'

He was a complete and utter pleasure to work

with, to be around, so much so that when Alison ducked into the staffroom for a ten-minute break later that morning, she wanted to turn tail and run, because it was just him in there and to be alone in his rather dazzling company rather terrified her.

'What about this...?'

She frowned as he handed her the local newspaper with an advertisement circled—a one-bedroom flat, two streets from the beach, and it wasn't that expensive. 'I've already seen it,' Alison admitted. 'It's above a pub that has live music six nights a week.' She sat down next to him. 'I did seriously think about it, though. Thanks,' she added. 'You didn't have to do that.'

'Can't help myself,' Nick admitted. 'I love looking at real estate—I've chosen the one I want...' And he showed her the stunning apartment he'd circled, with bay views and a balcony as big as the staffroom they were sitting in. 'Nice to dream.'

And it was, because Alison had circled the very same one in her own local newspaper, had looked it up on the net and taken a virtual tour of the place.

'You can't have it because it's already mine.'

'It's a great spot,' Nick said. 'I can absolutely see why you don't want to move away.'

And they got to talking, about she was on late shift tomorrow and she had to squeeze in two flat inspections beforehand, and there was a mixture of both relief and disappointment when he told her he was off for the weekend. Relief that he'd told a little white lie to Louise and the stab of disappointment Alison did her very best to ignore. Instead she told him how she loved to walk on the cliffs on her days off and, strange as it sounded, there was the most beautiful cemetery that he just had to explore, then about the coffee bar that did the ricotta cheese and cherry strudel which she rewarded herself with now and then. Then the intercom buzzed—someone searching for Nick—and Alison realised that her fifteen-minute break had turned into twenty-five.

'Told you.' Ellie smirked when she came round that evening on her way out for the night.

'Told me what?' Alison said, letting her in. There was no way she'd give Ellie so much as a hint that he'd won her over too, but Ellie was having none of it. Once she'd said hi to Rose, and chatted for a few minutes about an engagement present for a friend's party the following week, she asked to go on the computer.

'There!' Ellie was already a friend of his on Facebook—along with four hundred and thirty-seven others—and, yes, hanging upside down on a rope, his stomach looked lovely with his T-shirt around his neck. Alison did note that his status was single, and held her breath as she read about his crazy adventures—white-water rafting, rock-climbing, swimming in waterholes. And she didn't care if there were only freshwater crocodiles there, he was dangerous and reckless and everything she didn't want.

Great day at work—I love this place, Nick suddenly updated his status, and Alison blinked.

She thought of the toothaches and grumbles and moans down in section B and the drama with Ernest, which was pretty much routine in Emergency—it had been an okay day, even a good day perhaps, but hardly great.

Except, somehow he'd made it so.

Out to sample local delights, he added, and Alison rather hoped it wasn't Louise.

Ellie happily scrolled through what was just loads of chatter and comments from friends, and about a thousand photos.

'He broke off his engagement before he came here,' Ellie said knowledgeably.

'How do you know?'

'You can find out anything on this. Well, I'm not sure he broke it off, but I think so, and look…' Ellie was a machine and in no time at all had located photos of the once happy couple, but Alison had better things to do than fill her head with Nick.

'Come out with us,' Ellie pushed. 'Get some dinner…listen to a band.'

And Alison was about to again say no, she had to be up early for flat inspections and then work a late shift tomorrow, as Rose pointed out.

'There are a few of us meeting up.' Ellie smiled. 'You never know who'll be there.'

Which was a very good reason to decline, a very good reason to stay away, but instead of declining Alison gave her mum a smile.

'I'll be fine for tomorrow.' She tried not

to notice her mother's pursed lips as she left Ellie on the computer and headed to her room, straightening her already straight hair till it looked a little more *done* and pulling through some hair gloss, then putting on make-up as she changed from her shorts and T-shirt into something a little more dressy, but not too much. She checked her reflection in the mirror and tried to tone down the blusher on her cheeks before realising it was her own complexion.

'If you're going to be out late…' Rose came to her door.

'I'm not going to be late,' Alison said and then, unusually, she qualified a touch. 'But if I am, I'll give you a call.'

'You can't really stay out too long…' Rose didn't add the unspoken *You've got work...*

Alison didn't want to argue, she didn't want to point out again that she was twenty-four, that Ellie was on an early shift tomorrow and was still going out—that she had a life, that she wanted to live it…

Instead she crammed her ATM card, her mobile, some cash and her keys into a tiny bag and only when she had bitten back a smart retort did she look up.

'I'll let you know if I'm going to be late.' She gave her mum a kiss on the cheek and said goodnight then headed out to the cool, dark street and along to the bar, trying to join in with Ellie's easy chatter, but it was hard to be light-hearted when her mother made it such an effort to just go out. As she stepped into the bar, however, it wasn't her mother's veiled warning or an excess of blusher that had her cheeks pinking up again.

There was Moira and a few others, even Amy the registrar was sitting at the heavy wooden table. Making room for Ellie and Alison to join them, they ordered pizza. It wasn't at all unusual for the emergency crew to go out on a Friday night and, yes, Coogee was lovely and this bar was one hospital staff often frequented. It was just a rather good turnout from Emergency and Alison knew why—because coming back from the bar, balancing a jug of beer and some glasses with a bottle of water tucked under his arm, was the reason.

'Hey!' Nick gave her a smile and gave Ellie one too. This was her local, Alison told herself as she took a seat and glanced through the menu. She didn't just work nearby, she lived here, so more than anyone she had good reason to be there.

Except, Alison silently admitted, he was the real one.

CHAPTER TWO

EMERGENCY staff the world over knew how to have a good time when they were out, as Nick pointed out. Even the rather aloof Amy was letting her hair down and had had a dance, when she wasn't monopolising Nick.

'It's like a home from home!' Nick said to Alison as the table got louder and louder. 'Not that I regularly joined the Friday night out.'

'Too senior?' Alison asked.

'Too sombre,' Nick said, at least that was what she thought he said, because the music was really loud. 'Do you come here often?'

Alison grinned as, tongue in cheek, he delivered the cheesy line with a smile. 'I live five minutes away, but, no, not that often,' she admitted, because, well, it was true. 'I like the cafés and restaurants.' She didn't get to finish as Moira tottered over, a little the worse for wear, and tugged at Nick to go and dance. Alison didn't await his response, instead she disappeared through the beer garden and to the loo, where she stood for an inordinately long time, fiddling with her hair. Not that it made any difference but, ridiculously, she felt safer in there.

She could hear the thud-thud-thud of the band through the wall and it matched the thud-thud-thud of her heart, because she'd never, not once, found someone so instantly attractive. Oh, she knew she wasn't the only one, yet he was the only one—the only one who just on sight triggered something, just on voice confirmed it, just on scent…

'Moira…' Nick peeled the nurse's arm from around his neck with a smile. He was actually very good at letting a girl down gently, he'd had plenty of practice and though he'd enjoyed his holiday to date, the fun stopped when he started work—that sort of fun anyway. He took his work seriously, commanded respect and that was rather hard to come by the morning after a reckless night before. 'I don't dance.'

He didn't flee to the toilets like Alison had, but he made his way there, a little annoyed that he had come, but Amy had suggested it and it had seemed a bit rude to say no. He had sensed things were getting a little out of hand and had been about to head off, but had got talking to Alison and somehow forgotten that he was supposed to be heading for home.

And there she was, walking toward him right now, and here too was the very reason he hadn't headed for home when he should have.

'Hey.' He smiled down at her and she stopped walking. They stood in the beer garden amidst the noise and the chatter.

'I thought you were dancing.'

'Not for me.' He gave her a smile, but it was a wry one, a lying one, a strained one, because as the music tipped into something a little slower, he would at that very moment have danced, would have loved to do just that, because somehow she exceeded his limits, somehow he knew she could break his self-imposed rule, because all of a sudden work didn't matter.

'I'm just about to head off,' Alison admitted, because even if her stilettos seemed glued to the floor her heart was telling her to run.

'Do you want to go somewhere?' Nick's mouth said the words, though his brain insisted he shouldn't. 'Just us.' And Alison's eyes jerked down instead of up. Down to his forearm, to the blond hairs on it, to long-fingered hands that she wanted to wrap around hers. And maybe it was the overhead gas heaters in the beer garden, but the air was hot and her mind wasn't clear because with the pulse of the music and the laughter from beyond, it would, at that moment, have been so very easy to just be twenty-four.

To just be.

And, of course, just a moment later she recalled why she couldn't just be.

Alison looked up then to green eyes that awaited her response, that could never guess the inner turmoil inside her, who assumed, that for Alison, it was as easy as making a decision and grabbing her bag.

She shook her head and with good reason. Coogee was teeming with holidaymakers, with good-looking, testosterone-laden, 'here for a good time not a long time' males, and even if he was gorgeous, Nick could never be any different.

'No, thanks.'

'Hey, Nick!' Moira's radar located them and

rather unsteadily she teetered towards them. 'We're heading into town…'

Alison didn't wait to see if Nick was joining them. Instead she said goodnight, gathered her bag and walked, not along the street but along a beach that was dotted with small groups and some couples, and it was a relief to be out of there and a relief to be alone.

He *was* dangerous.

At least, he was to someone like her.

He had been flirting—oh, not anything major, but his glorious attention had homed in on her, more than a touch. She was quite sure that Nick did want to get to know her a little better—which, to Alison, just seemed pointless. He'd be gone in a few weeks, he was just there for some fun, which Alison didn't readily do.

Why, she asked herself as she walked along the beach she knew and loved, couldn't she be like Ellie, or Moira—just out there having fun, without worrying about tomorrow?

Her phone buzzed in her bag and she didn't need to check it to know it was from her mother. It was fifteen minutes after midnight after all.

'I just texted you!' Rose said as she walked in the door. 'I just wanted to know if you were going to be late.'

'I said I'd call if I was.'

'Well, it is after midnight.'

'Well, it is after midnight.' For a shadow of a second, she could almost hear Tim's voice, could almost picture her brother standing right where she was in the kitchen, good-naturedly teasing Rose when he came in late at night and Rose complained.

Except there had been Dad then to argue his case for him and, anyway, Tim had a way to him that always won their mum around.

God, but she missed him.

And her father too.

Missed, not just the people but the family they had been then, the security the others had provided, unnoticed at the time, the certainty they were there for each other, which had all been ripped away. So instead of a smart retort Alison looked instead at the fear in her mother's eyes and apologised for not texting and had a cup of tea and a chat with her mum, till Rose headed off for bed.

Then later, alone, when surely all her friends were still out, she went on the computer and checked her social network profile. She had one friend request and, yes, it was from Nick. He must befriend everyone, Alison decided, but she did click on his name, hoping for another little peek at his profile, except that, apart from his photo, all the rest of the photos and information were private.

She went to accept his friend request and for

a moment her finger hovered, then she chose to ignore it.

Very deliberately she ignored it, even if they did have eighteen mutual friends between them.

It was one a.m. on a Saturday after all.

A girl had some pride.

CHAPTER THREE

'ARE you okay?'

They were waiting for a multi-trauma at eight a.m. on Monday morning. The sky was black with a storm and the roads like ice after a long dry spell. Alison was in Resus this morning and so too was Nick. She'd said good morning at the bus stop, then moved to her regular seat. Ignored him in the staffroom that morning, her head buried in the crossword, but now they stood on opposite sides of the trauma bed, all set up and gowned up, waiting for the patients to arrive, though they were taking longer to get there than anticipated and Alison was quiet.

'I'm fine.'

'Look, about the other night...'

'What about the other night?' She frowned over her mask to him.

'I got waylaid by Moira and then you'd gone.'

'I'm not even thinking about that—I just hate getting kids in.'

Yes, it happened day in and day out, but some days you just hated it so and Nick, cool, confident Nick, actually coloured up a little bit, because for once, with a woman, it wasn't about him. He'd awoken slightly disconcerted on Saturday, and had spent the rest of the day trying ignore a niggle. He'd swum, walked for a while, but had ended up at a cemetery that was, strange as it might sound, both fascinating and beautiful, and then back to the flat, where that niggle had developed a name as he'd checked his social network profile and, no, she hadn't responded to that request either.

'ETA five minutes!' Sheila called, and he watched as Alison blinked twice.

'They're taking ages.'

'Rush-hour.'

'It's still ages.'

'It might not be that bad,' Nick said. 'We're set up for everything; we'll worry, if we need to, when they get here.'

It was actually very good advice and Alison gave a thin smile. 'Is that what you do?'

'I try to,' Nick replied. 'Right now I'm trying to work out seven down—begins with L, ends in E, recurring.'

'Life,' Alison said, and he grinned. 'I'm stuck on it too.'

'How's the flat-hunting?' he asked. 'Any luck?'

And she was about to shrug, to get back to worrying about the family that was coming in, but Nick was right. Until they arrived there was no point, so instead she followed his lead.

'Actually, yes!' She'd sworn not to get her hopes up, not to say a word, but she was so delighted she couldn't help herself. 'I got a phone call from a real estate agent about a flat, and though it's not officially on the market yet, he's arranging an inspection. It's within my price range and they want a quick sale… It all sounds a bit too good to be true.'

'It might be your time for some good luck.'

'How was the rest of your weekend?' Alison asked, because, well, she was interested and she wanted to get back to normal with him and he *was* so easy to talk to. 'Any surfing?'

'Well, I wouldn't quite call it surfing, but I did manage to get up and stay up for about half a second. It was great…' He stopped in mid-sentence as a siren blared the first ambulance's arrival. 'Okay,' Nick said, 'now we can get back to worrying.'

Her name was Polly and she was seven and petrified and on a trauma board, her head strapped down. She was so scared that she wasn't even crying.

'Hi, there, Polly.' Nick smiled down at her. 'I'm Nick, I'm a doctor. You're having a rotten morning, aren't you?' He spoke reassuringly to her as he rapidly examined her while Alison transferred the oxygen tubes. The paramedics had started an IV and were feeding information as they worked on. Alison was cutting off Polly's school uniform, attaching her to monitors and getting her observations.

'Where's my mum?' Her little teeth were chattering, just one thing on her mind, and Alison glanced over at Todd, the paramedic, who nodded his head towards the door and Alison went over.

'She's being cut out of the car,' Todd explained. 'She's conscious, but she's got some nasty cuts and is really agitated. She should be in soon. The police are trying to get hold of Dad.'

'Thanks,' Alison said, but nothing else, and headed back to Polly. 'Mum will be coming in soon, and we're getting hold of Dad, but right now we need to make sure you're okay.'

Amazingly she appeared to be.

There were some minor cuts and bruises, but she was neurologically sound and her abdomen was soft and non-tender. After a thorough examination and some cervical spine films, they peeled off the board and beneath it was a little girl who was a bit calmer, but still shaky, asking after her mum and very worried about her dad.

'He's got an interview.' Now Polly did start crying.

'Hey,' Nick said, 'don't worry about that. Your dad will be so relieved that you're okay.' Except the little girl could not be consoled.

'Can I move her over to a cubicle?' Alison

checked with Nick, and then spoke away from Polly. 'Mum's about to arrive…'

'Sure, just…' He didn't finish, and Alison didn't wait to find out or to be told—yes, she would keep a very close eye on Polly.

She could see Todd hanging around, taking ages to sort out the blankets, and she deliberately ignored him. Alison didn't like him. He was good at his job and everything but he had asked her out a few times and didn't know how to take no for an answer. He'd also been out with half the department, and expected Alison to follow suit.

'Hey, Alison.' Todd came over. 'How is she?'

'Fine,' Alison answered. 'We're just about to move her out of Resus.'

'How are you?'

'Fine,' came her reply, but she didn't elaborate, actually refusing to speak to him about anything other than work.

She was glad she had moved Polly out, though her mum's sobs still reached the cubicle and after rechecking the little girl's obs, Alison didn't try to placate her. 'I'll go and find out how she is.'

The police were outside in the corridor and they brought Alison up to speed on things before she went in. Ellie and Sheila, the unit manager, were helping Nick and Alison observed for a moment before asking how she was doing.

'She's got a nasty arm laceration that needs to go straight to Theatre,' Ellie said. 'She's hysterical. Nick's told her that her little girl's okay.'

'This is the nurse looking after Polly,' Nick told his patient, and Alison went over to the distraught woman. 'Rebecca,' he added, and Alison nodded.

'I'm looking after Polly,' Alison said. 'She's doing really well. As soon as you're more settled you can see her.'

'David?'

'Your husband?' Alison checked. 'I've just spoken to the police and he's on his way in.'

'He'll be so worried.'

'I'll look out for him,' Alison promised. 'I'll speak to him the second he arrives and I'll bring him in to Polly and to you just as soon as I can.'

'He'll be—'

'I'll look after him,' Alison said gently. 'Try not to worry.'

'Where are they?' The man, who was chalk-white and looked as if he might pass out any second, needed no introduction. Alison knew this must be the father. A security man was running in behind him, about to tell him to move his car, but Alison dealt with practicalities, got the keys from him and asked for permission for Security to move it. David was really in no state to drive.

'They're going to be okay,' Alison said, and guided him straight to a side room. 'Let me just talk to you for a moment and then I'll take you in to see Polly.' She knew he needed to see his daughter, but in the state he was in, he would just upset Polly more.

'Polly's escaped lightly,' Alison explained. 'She's got some cuts and a few bruises across her chest and to her shoulder from the seat belt, but she's talking and she's fine.'

'Rebecca?'

'She's got a nasty arm laceration and they're talking about taking her straight to Theatre. There might be some concussion and they're going to arrange for a head CT. She's very distressed, they had to cut her out of the car, but she knows where she is and what's happened, and she's very worried about Polly and about you.'

'Oh, God.' He bunched his hands by his head

and took in some deep breaths. 'I thought the worst…'

'Of course you did,' Alison said gently. 'We were prepared for the worst too, but they do seem to be relatively okay. I'll get the doctor to speak to you just as soon as he can.'

'I don't think I even said goodbye this morning. I've got a job interview today…' Alison frowned, because she'd heard Polly going on about it. 'I was so worked up about it, I can't even remember if I said goodbye…' And he broke down then and Alison listened and found out that he had lost his job nine months ago, that he had, in fact, had a nervous breakdown and was still struggling to deal with things, but was slowly picking up. And because she listened she heard too that today was a vital day, so much hope had been pinned on it, that this job had meant everything, right up till this point. She could understand now how upset Rebecca would be, not about the job but about her husband's reaction.

'Let me take you in to Polly,' Alison said when he had calmed down. 'And I'll let your wife know that you're here.'

He did really well, he smiled and said all the right things to Polly—that the interview didn't matter a scrap, just as long as she and her mother were okay, that they would be fine, that they were all going to be fine. Rarely for Alison, she felt a sting of tears at the backs of her eyes and left them to it to go and speak with the wife.

'Hi, Rebecca.' Alison came in as Nick and the trauma surgeons looked at the patient's arm, and though Nick was concentrating, he still heard her speak. 'Polly's fine, her dad's with her—and he's fine. He really is okay.' Rebecca started crying and bizarrely for a second it sounded to Nick as if it was the husband who was hurt. 'I've told him that when the surgeons have finished looking at your arm I'll bring him in to see you. Rebecca, he's holding up really well.' And the arm Nick was holding down for the surgeons to assess relaxed just a little bit beneath his fingers.

'David's told me all that's been going on,' Alison continued, 'and, honestly, now that he knows you two are going to be okay, he really is fine.'

'He can't cope with things,' Rebecca said, and it was the first proper conversation she'd managed since her arrival.

'Not the little things perhaps,' Alison said, and stroked the poor woman's cheek. 'But he's dealing well with this. Maybe he's finding out he's stronger than he thinks.'

'So much hinges on today…'

'I know.' She glanced up at Nick. 'David had an important job interview today,' Alison explained, then looked back at the patient. 'When things are more settled we could ring the company and explain what's happened.' She paused and hoped, not wanting to presume but grateful when he stepped in.

'I'm happy to do that,' Nick said.

'That's good,' Alison said to Rebecca. 'It will sound better coming from a doctor.' And Nick looked down at his patient and saw her close her eyes in relief, felt her body relax and he realised that head CT wasn't quite so urgent.

'There's a lot of stress going on for them,' Alison murmured to Nick. 'They really didn't need this.'

'Thanks,' Nick said. He realised he'd learned something, and whatever it was he decided he would process it later.

As Ellie prepared Rebecca for Theatre, knowing what would put his patient's mind at rest more than any medication, Nick made the phone call Alison had suggested, then returned to tell the couple how it had gone. 'They were really grateful for you letting them know,' Nick told David. 'Especially with all that's going on. They've asked you to ring later in the day or tomorrow if you get a chance to arrange another time. They sound pretty keen,' he added, then glanced up as Alison came in with a nervous Polly.

'Here's Mum,' Alison said, and Rebecca and Polly had a kiss and a cuddle before Rebecca was taken to Theatre, because only seeing her mum would truly reassure the anxious child.

'I'm going to take her up to the children's ward soon,' Alison told Rebecca. 'Just for observation. They'll make a fuss of her. You can ring her this evening when you're back from Theatre and feeling better—or one of the staff might bring her up for a little visit.'

'She's nice…' Rebecca said when Alison had

left. Nick agreed, saying that Polly was being well looked after by her, then told his patient to put her oxygen mask back on because he didn't want to think about how nice Alison was—there was more to Alison than there was time to know, more to her than there was scope to explore. No, he really didn't need this.

Heading into the staffroom for a quick lunch break later, when Ellie asked if he was going to the social club that night, it would have been far more sensible to answer that gleam in her eye with a smile and a 'Yes', or take Moira up on that offer to go to that Irish pub, because instinct told him that they knew the rules—that he was on holiday and not here for a long time, just a good one, but instead all he *really* noticed was that Alison had glasses on today while doing the crossword and didn't look up to hear his response, though her cheeks burnt red and her ears were pink as she pretended to concentrate on the puzzle in front of her. Because the seat next to her was the only one left, he chose it, peered over her shoulder and, yes, she was stuck on the same word as he'd been. He was about to nudge her, to tease her, because 'leitmotif' was a word it had taken him a full morning to get, but he deliberately stopped himself.

'Leitmotif!' He heard the triumph in her voice and ignored it, felt the haste of her pen beside him, and it took every bit of effort not to turn round and join her in that moment.

No, *this* Nick really didn't need.

CHAPTER FOUR

'ALISON doesn't want to be my friend.'

He lasted two days.

Two days trying not to notice how her neck went a little bit pink when he spoke to her. Two days ignoring the fragrance of her hair when their heads occasionally met over a patient, or that now and then she'd rub her forehead and on would come her glasses. Two days of just talking, just keeping it as it was, then, as happened at times, but had to happen on this day, Alison came off the worse for wear with an inebriated patient. Showered and changed into the most threadbare, faded scrubs, Nick got the most astonishing view of what appeared to be a purple bra and panties, before Sheila pointed the problem out and Alison put on a theatre gown. Like a dressing gown over pyjamas, Nick thought, and then tried not to think, and then just stopped thinking for a dangerous moment as she sat next to him writing up his notes, her ponytail wet and heavy, and he forgot, just simply forgot not to flirt.

'Why don't you want to be my friend, Alison?' He nudged her as if they were sitting in a classroom and Alison, who wasn't having the greatest day, annoyed with herself for not replacing her spare uniform, found herself trying not to smile, yet she did carry on the joke and put her arm over the notes she was writing as if he was trying to copy her.

'I am your friend, Nick.'

'Not on Facebook…'

'I haven't got time to *play* online…' Alison said. 'Some of us live and work in the real world—I'm studying to get on this trauma course.'

'You're friends with Ellie.' He grinned and then stopped, and so too did Alison. There was this charge in the air; it would be far safer to carry on writing, or just get up and go, but she didn't, she just sat. 'Are you going to have to get the bus wearing that? Only I can—'

'I washed my uniform and begged them on the rehab ward to use their tumbledryer…' She didn't get to finish because screams filled the department and Nick jumped up as a man was stretchered in, sucking on the gas, in sheer agony at the prospect of being moved from the stretcher to the gurney.

'Can I have a quick look before you move him?'

His jeans had already been cut off and it was a rather horrible sight, his dislocated patella causing the whole leg to look deformed. It was an excruciating injury and Alison blinked as, without X-ray, without delay, Nick told the man to suck on the gas and with one flick popped it back.

A shriek filled the department and then a sob and then the sound of relieved silence.

'Let's get him on the gurney and then we'll need X-rays.' He chatted for a moment to his extremely grateful patient, then chatted a bit more to the rather impressed paramedics, then he walked over to where Alison was now on the computer, checking some blood results, and she could feel the heat whoosh up her neck as he came over.

'God, I'm good.' He grinned and, yes, it was arrogant, but it was funny too, and Alison couldn't help but smile as she rolled her eyes.

'Yeah, but you know it.'

He looked at her and he wanted to look away, to walk away, to remember he was there for reasons other than this, except there was something about Alison that was hard to resist. Something about her that meant stern warnings could so easily be ignored.

'Hey…' Moira dashed past '…are you coming to the beach later, Alison?' She gave a hopeful glance at Nick. 'There are a few of us going—Amy…'

'Not for me,' Alison said.

'Or me!' Nick said. Moira shrugged and moved on. It was like sugar to artificial sweetener, Nick decided, because sugar was something he was trying to give up too. Yes, sweeteners tasted okay, once you got used to them, and for a while there they sufficed, but sooner rather than later you went back for the real thing…. And maybe he should just go to the beach, or a bar, or just home and have that takeaway that Amy had offered. Instead he found himself asking Alison if she wanted to go for a coffee.

'I've got a dentist appointment.'

'Ouch.' He pulled a sympathetic face. 'Hope it's not too painful.'

'Oh, it's just my six-monthly check-up.' And she smiled, but it sort of faded as she turned back to the computer, because it just about summed her up.

She *had* six-monthly check-ups, and when this one was done, no doubt, she'd do as she always did and while she was there make an appointment for the next one and write it in her diary, and she'd be there—she never missed.

Same as her eight-weekly trim at the hairdresser's.

Same as she booked in the dog to be shampooed and clipped.

She bet Nick hadn't spent ages on the computer, researching dentists to ensure he didn't miss his six-monthly check-up.

The most gorgeous, sexy man was asking

her for coffee and she'd turned him down for a dental appointment!

'We could meet up afterwards, but not for long, I've got to look at that flat.' She could hear her own words and inwardly reeled at them, and even as she mistyped the patient's UR number she sounded almost blasé as she dipped in her toe and felt only warmth. 'So long as I don't end up getting a filling or something.'

'Let's just hope you've been flossing.'

She had been.

Alison lay in the chair with her mouth open as the dentist tapped each tooth in turn.

Not a single filling.

Again.

He cleaned them, polished them and they felt like glass as she ran her tongue over them. As she paid and headed out, she didn't get why she was so nervous.

Why she wanted to just not show up.

Because it might just be coffee and strudel and then she'd be disappointed, Alison thought as she stepped out onto the street with her sparkly clean teeth. Or, worse, it might be more than coffee and strudel…

Maybe that was what he did—pick someone wherever he went, dazzle her with the full glare of his spotlight.

And he really could dazzle.

Since two minutes past six on Friday morning, he'd been on her mind.

She rang her mum, told her she was having coffee with friends before she went to look at the flat, and as she turned the corner he was there already and looked up and smiled as she made her way over and took her seat at the pavement café.

'How was the dentist?'

'Fine,' Alison said, 'I've earned my strudel.'

He ordered, and her nerves disappeared because, absolutely, he was still easy to talk to and easy to listen to, too. Not working for a few months, Nick said, was the single best thing he had ever done. 'Because,' he continued, spooning *four* sugars into his coffee as Alison tapped in a sweetener, 'I actually missed it.'

'Well, you love your job,' Alison said. 'That's obvious.'

'But I didn't,' Nick said, and Alison blinked at his admission. 'That's one of the reasons I took a year off. I wasn't even sure if I wanted to do medicine any more, let alone work in Emergency.'

'But you seem to enjoy it.'

'I'm starting to.' He was in no rush, just sat and drank his coffee as if he'd be happy to sit there all evening and told her a little about himself. 'There was never any question that I'd be a doctor—preferably a surgeon. My dad's one, my grandfather was one, my elder brother is, as is my sister…' He rolled his eyes. 'Can you imagine what we talk about over dinner?'

'What about your mum?'

'Homework monitor,' Nick said, and Alison laughed. 'There was no question and, really, I accepted that, right up till the last year of medical school—which I enjoyed, but…' He shrugged. 'I don't know, I wanted to take a year off to travel, but I ended up taking an internship.'

'I was the same,' Alison interrupted, which was rare for her. Normally she sat quietly and listened. 'I wanted a year off when I finished school, but Mum and Dad said I should finish my studies.'

'I had the same conversation with mine.' Nick groaned. 'So I did my internship, decided I liked emergency work, met Gillian and it was all…'

'Nice,' Alison offered.

And they could hardly hear the other's story for telling their own, or hardly tell their own for hearing the other person's.

'Work was okay about it—they gave me a year's unpaid leave, but they made it pretty clear that there'd be no extension. I've no idea how bad divorce must be,' Nick said, 'because breaking up after four years was hard enough. I mean, there was no real reason—it was just the talk of mortgages and babies and if we'd hyphenate our names…' He called the waiter and ordered another coffee and Alison ordered a hot chocolate. 'I was having a midlife crisis apparently!' Nick said. 'At thirty!'

'I had one too,' Alison said, 'and I'm only twenty-four.' And she laughed, for the first time she laughed about the sorry situation she had found herself in a year ago. She told him a little about Paul, her one serious relationship—how well he'd got on with her mother, how hard it had been to end it—but there was something she wanted to know about him. 'So…' Alison was cautious, but terribly, terribly curious. 'Are you two having a break…?'

'No,' Nick said. 'I ended it and it wasn't nice, but it was necessary. I just hope one day she can see that—four weeks later I'd got a round-the-world ticket and was flying to New York.'

And she sat outside a pavement café with a man who came from the other side of the world, but who felt somehow the same, and there was a fizz in her veins she'd never felt before, a glow inside as they chatted on, and she could have stayed and spoken to him for hours, except she had her real estate appointment at seven.

'Do you want me to come?' Nick asked. 'I love looking at houses.'

'It's an apartment.'

'It's someone else's!' Nick grinned. 'I love being nosy.'

And Alison smiled back because, even if flat-hunting was hell, yes, she liked that aspect of it too, loved that peek into others' lives, the solace that wardrobes the length and breadth of Coogee were filled fit to bursting, that some people didn't even make their beds when they had people coming round to view. And she told him so and told him some more. 'One couple were rowing on Saturday,' Alison said.

'The owners?' Nick asked, and she loved how his eyes widened in glee.

'I think they were breaking up.' Alison nodded. 'They stood on the balcony and had this screaming match during the open inspection.'

'God, I wish I'd been there,' Nick said, and she kind of wished he'd been there too—liked that he liked the same things as her, that odd little things pleased.

'Come on, then.' She went to fish out her

purse, but Nick waved her away and it would have been embarrassing really to protest—and even there he was different. Paul had decided on their first date that equality meant you split the bill—and she told him so as they walked down the hill and turned at the chemist's.

'He lived in constant terror that he might end up paying for a round of garlic bread when he hadn't eaten a slice,' Alison said, and then wondered if she should have said that, if it was bitchy to talk about your ex like that. 'He was a great guy, just toward the end…' She trailed off and Nick got it, he just completely got it.

'Gillian and I ended up the same,' he said as they walked up the hill to meet the real estate agent. 'At first I used to love it that she did my crossword, but near the end I was setting my alarm early and nearly breaking my neck to get down the stairs and to the newspaper first.' He glanced over to check that she got it too and

Alison smiled. 'It's not the crossword, or the garlic bread, is it?'

'He was great,' Alison said. 'It was more…' And she told him a bit about herself, not enough to have him running in the opposite direction, just a little. 'It was too nice,' Alison said. 'Too easy, almost. Mum's a bit over-protective and he didn't seem to mind… In fact, Paul suggested he move in.' She still burnt at the memory. 'Mum was delighted, it felt like they had it all worked out.'

'They just forgot to ask you,' Nick said, and for the first time in her life, she felt as if someone got her.

CHAPTER FIVE

ALISON had very few expectations as the real estate agent opened the front door and she stepped inside. There had been so many disappointments, so many let-downs, that, in the name of self-preservation, she kept her hopes determinedly down.

Even as they looked at the surprisingly spacious lounge, even that this apartment actually had a kitchen, though even the real estate agent managed a wry smile at the supposed glimpse of the bay. Nick could see it because he was a full foot taller, but apparently, there at the top right hand side of the kitchen window was her beloved beach.

'There is a second bedroom.' Alison peered

into a cupboard. 'Well,' the real estate agent attempted, 'it would make a nice nursery.'

'Or study,' Nick offered when Alison laughed, and then they moved along the hall.

'This is the main bedroom.'

It was larger than expected too, and, really, all Alison's wishes had been answered. The owners were off to London, the husband leaving the next day apparently, and the wife following in a month's time. 'Really, he'd like to know it was all taken care of before he leaves,' the real estate agent explained. 'They want a thirty-day settlement…'

And she listened to the wah-wah white noise as the agent did his spiel, but it wasn't the large airy bedroom Alison could see but the suitcase beside the bed, and it truly dawned that if she bought this flat, she was, without doubt, saying goodbye to her dream of travelling, and even though she'd thought it through, even though she'd gone over it a hundred million times, when it came to it, she stalled at the final hurdle.

'Can I have till the morning?' Alison saw the agent's eyebrows rise in surprise. For weeks he had seen her at open inspections at places far less nice than this and now he was almost handing her this opportunity on a plate and at the last minute the *genuine buyer* he'd ensured the vendors he had was faltering.

'The vendors want to save on advertising, that's why I agreed to bring you through, but the photographer is booked for midday and it will go on the market then, unless I hear otherwise.'

'Sure,' Alison said. 'I'll ring tomorrow.'

'I'm impressed,' Nick said as they walked down the street.

'Why?'

'I thought you'd snatch his hand off to get it—you certainly know how to play it cool.'

'It's not that,' Alison started, and then halted herself. She was hardly going to tell a virtual stranger, albeit a very nice virtual stranger, her dilemma—and then, in that moment she realised the stark truth, it wasn't even a dilemma. She really had no choice in the matter. 'I just want to speak to Mum first.'

'It's a big decision,' Nick said, and Alison stopped walking.

'I turn off here.' She gave him a nice smile. 'Thanks for the coffee.'

'Thanks for the company.'

It was a strange moment. The lightheartedness of earlier had gone—Alison heavy with indecision and Nick no doubt not understanding why.

'I'll see you at work tomorrow.'

She turned up the street and bizarrely felt like

crying. She knew, was positive in fact, that he was watching her and that made her walk faster. She wanted to turn, wanted to run back to him, to go to a club or a bar, to ask him about his adventures, she wanted to sit and listen to music, to be late, to not go home. Instead she turned the key in the door.

'Hi, Mum.'

'I was just starting to get worried.'

'It's not even eight!' Alison pointed out.

'You said you were out for coffee,' Rose said. 'A quick phone call would have been nice…'

There was a retort on Alison's tongue, an urge to yet again point out her age, another beginning to a row that had never taken place but one they were steadily building towards. Then Alison caught sight of her father and brother's photo on the shrine that used to be a mantelpiece, and swallowed down her bitter response, knew this was the small price she paid for living, knew she would do her best to avoid arguing and knew for certain that she had to move out.

'I went to look at that flat.' She saw her mother's rapid blink. 'I think I've finally found one.' She spoke quickly into the ensuing silence. 'It's a ten-minute walk away, it's got everything—two bedrooms, even a little balcony…' And she waited for her mother to fill in the gap, to point out that she could live here for nothing, that it was stupid, pointless, but for once Rose didn't speak, and not for the first time Alison tried to be honest. 'I don't know if I should take it. I mean, I'll have a mortgage, there's no way I'd be able…' She glanced up and saw Rose swallow. 'You know I always wanted to travel…'

And Rose in that moment had a choice between the lesser of two evils. She must have, because for once she didn't jump in with all the reasons Alison would be stupid to leave home;

for the first time ever she bordered on enthusiastic about her daughter moving out.

'It sounds a nice flat.' There was a wobble to Rose's voice. 'Two bedrooms, you say?'

'Well, only one that's actually big enough for a bed, but the other could be a nice study.'

'You'll need a study if you do your trauma course.'

'The thing is, Mum—'

'I know you want to travel…' Rose broke in. 'I've been thinking. I've given it a lot of thought, actually. We deserve a treat.' As Alison opened her mouth to protest, Rose overrode her. 'I know you've always wanted to go to Bali. I wouldn't mind seeing it too… My treat,' she said loudly as Alison tried to interrupt.

And as she lay in her single bed later on, Alison tried not to cry. She felt horribly selfish actually, because in the space of a few hours she'd found a flat and been offered a fortnight's trip to Bali. It was just…

The first year after the accident she'd taken her mum for weekends away, she and Paul had taken her for a holiday once too, with Alison sharing a room with her mum. Then last year they'd been to Queensland for a week—her mum saying all the time how much her father and brother would have liked it.

She ripped back the sheet, and almost ran to the window.

There were no bay views from her bedroom but there was the distant roar of the ocean as she pushed the window open and gulped in the cool night air. And there were the sounds of the bars and the backpackers and youth and fun, and she was tempted to run down in her nightdress, tempted to find what ever bar Nick was in, to rush up to him and kiss his face off, to take him by the hand and dance and dance, to come back at dawn *without* sending her mother a text.

To be free.

CHAPTER SIX

'YAY!' The whole staffroom cheered when a beaming Alison revealed her news as she walked into her late shift.

She'd soon got over herself—a brisk walk on the beach at the crack of dawn and a stern talk with herself had turned things round in her head. Then, at nine a.m. she'd rung the real estate agent, at nine-forty she'd been at the bank, at nine fifty-five she'd handed the deposit over and signed a mountain of forms, and now, at midday, she almost had a mortgage.

'Congratulations.' Nick pulled her aside the first chance he got. It had been a busy afternoon and Alison had been working the paediatric cots while Nick had been in Resus, but as she came back from her coffee break, he was just heading off for his.

'Thanks!' Alison said. 'It's pretty exciting.'

'How about dinner,' Nick offered, 'to celebrate?' And when she paused, when she didn't just jump in and say yes, Nick upped the offer. 'With lots of garlic bread.'

'Why?' He didn't understand the hurt in her eyes, he didn't really understand the question. 'Why would we go out for dinner?'

'Because you want to?' Nick said, because he was sure that she did. 'Because I want to?'

'I don't…' Her voice trailed off, and her words hung in the air, the wrong words because she did want to, very much. She had been about to say that she didn't see the point in pursuing this, except when he was around she did see the point—he was nice and funny and whatever attraction was, it was there, for both of them.

'I'm not sure.' She changed tack, headed for

safer ground, used a method far safer than exposing her heart. 'What with work and everything.'

Nick could have pointed out that it was just dinner, that, given they'd been out on Friday, clearly work colleagues did meet up outside the walls of Emergency. Except it wasn't just dinner and it wasn't the emergency crew he wanted to see more of out of hours—it was her. And, yes, he was bending his own rules, but it was, after all, just for a short while and even if it was work, it was still a holiday. He wasn't asking for for ever, he wasn't threatening to run away with her heart, he just wanted more of the smile that sometimes brightened her serious face, wanted more of the woman he was getting to know.

'We could keep it quiet.' He ran a hand through his hair as he renegotiated his own boundaries.

'Sounds good.'

And those words were the bravest she'd uttered.

'About ten?' Nick said, and her smile disappeared when she realised he meant tonight, that his impulsive world was invading hers. 'Ten-thirty?' he said, and named a nice bar. 'I'll pick you up.' And she thought of her mother and shook her head at the image.

'Ten-thirty's great.' She forced a smile. 'I'll meet you there.'

Thankfully, she was kept almost busy enough not to be nervous. It wasn't a date, she kept telling herself, it was just friends going out for a couple hours. She managed not to think about it, especially when dealing with a very restless baby and an extremely anxious mum.

'She's putting on weight.' Lucia, the paediatric intern, was thorough and nice and doing her best to reassure Shelly, the mother of an eight-week-old. 'I know reflux babies are hard, but you are doing everything right.' And she went through all the medications and thickeners that little Casey was on, and checked that she was being positioned properly.

'She won't settle, though,' Shelly said. 'She hardly goes two hours.'

'That's why my registrar suggested you look at the mother and baby day clinic,' Lucia said. 'She's well, though.' Despite everything, the baby was well. There were no signs of dehydration, her nappies were wet, her obs were normal—she was just a very fussy baby. 'You've got an appointment coming up with the paediatrician…' Her pager was going off, her registrar had already looked over the baby and deemed little Casey well enough to go home, and there was only one paediatric bed left to last the night. Lucia was only checking her over again because the mother was still concerned, and despite Lucia's reassurances, as she said goodbye Alison knew Shelly wasn't reassured. Neither was she, though her concern wasn't just for the baby. She could see Shelly's shaking hands as she did up the poppers on her baby's little outfit, saw that despite the baby screaming, Shelly said nothing to soothe her, just wrapped her up and put her in her little car seat, without a word, without a cuddle. There was no malice in her actions. She was just a mother very close to the edge.

'Amy saw this baby and handed her over to Paeds.' She handed Nick the notes. 'Amy's gone home and Paeds have seen the baby and they're happy to discharge. I'm just concerned…' She waited as he read through the notes, waited for him to roll his eyes, or sigh, or say 'I'll get to it,' but instead he listened as Alison voiced her concerns and he read easily between the lines. 'Lucia did suggest the day clinic to sort out her sleeping pattern.'

'What did Mum say to that?'

'She agreed to it, but there's normally a two-week wait.'

'Do you think she's depressed?'

'I'm sure she is,' Alison said, 'just not enough for an urgent admission. And frankly I'd be feeling depressed. I tried feeding her and it was hard work.'

'Okay.' He slid off his stool and went over and introduced himself. He chatted to Shelly about her babe, taking her out of her little seat and examining the infant himself. 'When is she due for a feed?'

'She's constantly due!' Shelly said through gritted teeth. 'She never finishes a bottle, she screams as if I'm pouring acid down her throat instead of milk…' The young mother bit back angry tears as her baby lay on the mattress, screaming. 'I know she's got reflux, I know it will get better…'

'Okay,' Nick said, and when Shelly didn't, Alison started to dress the baby again. She waited for him to suggest she get a bottle, that he observe the babe feed, or a little bit more of what had taken place on and off for the last four hours, but he did none of that. He gave a brief smile and nodded and said he'd be back in a moment as Shelly blew out a long breath.

'What's happening?'

'I'm not sure,' Alison said, as the baby's screams quadrupled. 'Here,' she said, when Shelly sat down beside the cot and put her head in her hands, 'would you like me to take Casey for a little walk? I'll see if I can find out what's happening.'

Casey did stop crying, the motion, the bright lights, the activity all distracting her enough as Alison walked through the department and found Nick perched back on his stool.

'What's happening?'

'She'll be admitted,' Nice said. 'I've just paged the paed reg.'

'He's happy for her to go home and be seen in Outpatients…'

'Well, I'm not,' Nick said. 'Which means that she's going to be admitted.'

And he told the paediatric reg the same when he picked up the phone. Yes, he was friendly and perfectly reasonable at first, and then Alison got her first glimpse of a different Nick, an extremely assertive Nick who, despite the smile and the easygoing banter, took his job very seriously and would not be argued with.

A Nick who was going to go far.

'It's not even an option,' Nick said, turning his pen over and over between the desk and his fingers, clearly in no rush. 'She can be transferred to another hospital if there are no beds here, but I'm not happy to send her home, so either ring your intern and tell her to come and do the paperwork, or I can ring your consultant to discuss it further. But whatever comes of it, this baby isn't going home.'

'That told them,' Alison said.

'I don't see why everything has to be an argument—it's the same everywhere,' Nick added. 'I know there are hardly any beds, I know she's not acute, but…' He glanced down towards the bay. 'I'm going to have a word with Mum.'

He was nice and practical and explained that Casey should be monitored and was upfront about Shelly's tension. 'We need to be really sure we haven't overlooked anything and if everything checks out, we need to make sure you get the support you need with Casey.'

He just dealt with things, without fuss or drama, and he didn't moan as he did so.

'He's nice, that doctor,' Shelly commented as Alison took her up to the ward, the porter wheeling the mother and baby in a chair.

'He is,' Alison agreed, and then she remembered.

She was having dinner with that nice doctor tonight.

* * *

Taking the bus simply wasn't an option. By the time she had taken Shelly up to the ward *and* dashed back, it was already well after nine and she'd missed her bus, and as much as Nick might be expecting her to change quickly and dash back out, and as much as Alison wanted to look as if she'd changed quickly and dashed back out, there was no girl facing such a prospect who would. Which was why, despite now being a responsible, soon-to-be homeowner, Alison splurged on a taxi, though she made sure that it dropped her off at the end of the street to avoid even more questions from her mum.

'Out?' Rose frowned as Alison flew in the door.

'For dinner,' Alison said. 'To celebrate getting the flat.'

'Who with?'

'Friends from work,' Alison said, and it wasn't

a lie, she consoled herself as she dashed up the stairs. It was just a slight exaggeration, or rather playing the situation down, because friends from work was safe, a friend from work a bit different.

A male friend from work.

A gorgeous, blond, funny, sexy, 'here for a good time, not a long time' male friend from work.

Getting ready for Nick was rather like getting a patient quickly prepared for Theatre. Alison went through a rapid mental checklist, cleaning her teeth, shaving her legs, even cleaning her ears, body lotion, perfume, subtle make-up, hair gloss, nice underwear, really, really nice underwear—not that he'd be seeing it, but just because, because, because…

She was simply meeting a friend from work, Alison told herself over and over as she trawled through her wardrobe till the contents lay on a heap on her bed, wondering how she could have nothing to wear when her entire bed was covered. She settled for a pale grey tube skirt that she'd had for ever and a cheap but cheerful top she'd bought the previous week, pulled on some bracelets as she dashed downstairs, wished her mum goodnight and flew down the street, rather surprised to find Nick waiting for her at the end.

'Don't want you walking on your own.'

'I do it all the time,' Alison said.

'You look nice.' His eyes told her that he meant it.

'Oh.' She gave a casual shrug, one that said it had been no effort at all! 'Thanks.'

He was just a friend, Alison told herself as he went to kiss her on the cheek.

Or maybe not, because very deliberately he avoided her cheek and met her mouth, and it was slow and deliberate and its meaning was clear, crystal clear, that this was more than just friendship.

And for Nick it was confirmation too.

He felt first her hesitancy, her guardedness and then he felt what he knew, or rather had guessed at. Felt this gathering of passion on full lips and despite self-issued warnings he wanted to unleash it.

'Just so we don't spend the whole night wondering,' Nick said, and pulled back, even though he wanted more. And she smiled because now, instead of wondering, she knew.

So she kissed him, just to confirm it, and despite Nick's best-laid plans, now they would spend the whole night not just wondering but wanting too, because one taste of his tongue and Pandora's box opened and it was passion that slithered out. Alison could feel the press of brick wall on her back, feel the silk of his hair on her fingers, and ten doors from prison he turned the key and she flew, her body just flew to his, met his, wanted his, and she'd never kissed or been kissed like this, his hands on her hips and his mouth drinking hers. And it was absolutely right that he stop, that he look into her eyes, pupils so dilated he might have put in atropine drops, and she watched him taste his own lips, taste her again and try to get his breath.

'Let's eat,' Nick said.

Let's not, Alison wanted to reply as his forehead met hers as they rested just a moment to regroup, because, as Alison had just found out, kisses changed things.

Good ones especially.

Their restaurant was chosen by the delicious herby scent that wafted onto the street, and it was Italian. Alison chose giant ravioli in a creamy mushroom sauce and Nick didn't skimp on the garlic bread either.

It was different from any other date she'd been on because there was neither awkwardness nor ease, or rather there was, just not in the usual rhythm.

There was ease to the conversation, it was the table between them that made things awkward—just watching each other's mouths as they ate, that made them tense.

'Is everything okay?' The waiter checked when, plates quickly cleared, Nick asked for the bill.

'I'll get dinner next time,' Alison said when he paid, and it was as assured as that, for both of them, that there would be a next time.

'Your wine.' The waiter handed them their half-bottle and Nick smiled at the little differences around the world, because till a few minutes ago they could have been anywhere. Walking out of the restaurant with wine in hand, they saw the show of the ocean endlessly unfolding, the night warm, the sky thick with stars. Yes, it was late, but too early to end their evening, and a walk on the beach was cleansing after the noise in the restaurant. 'Do you want to come back for coffee?' Nick said, and then he winced a bit. 'I do mean coffee.'

Alison would have loved to because she wanted more of him and a coffee would be nice too, except she couldn't.

'I really have to get back soon.' She hadn't dared check her phone. 'I've got loads on tomorrow.'

So instead they sat and Nick had a mouthful from the bottle and so too did Alison and, yes, she was home, but it felt like paradise.

She stared out at the stars and there were millions of them. The more she looked the more she could see, and she wished she could read them, wished she could point to a constellation, and she told him that. 'I'm going to do an astronomy course one day.'

'Never interested me,' Nick admitted, 'till I came to Australia. I've never seen stars like it.'

And they lay back on the sand and just stared, and she could have lain there for ever, but she really did have to get back and she told him, well, not quite the truth but a little bit more than she had previously—that her mum would be starting to worry.

'Why don't you ring her if she'll be worrying?' came Nick's practical suggestion, because for most twenty-four-year-olds a phone call would suffice.

'And tell her what?' Alison dodged the issue. 'That I'm lying on a beach and I'm worried that he's going to kiss me, because I really don't think I'll be able to stop?'

'I'm worried this time too,' Nick said, and her heart twisted as they spoke their own shorthand, that he remembered her words as she remembered his.

'I have visions,' Alison admitted, turning from the stars to his lovely, lovely face, and for some reason she felt free to be just a little more honest. 'Of me at forty, or fifty, and I'm a lot larger than I am now, I've got a big shiny red face and I'm a virgin, and it's Tuesday and Mum's serving me dinner at the table—beef stroganoff...'

And he didn't leap from the beach and run. He just smiled and rolled over on his side and his hand moved and toyed without thinking with the bottom of her skirt, because her admission brought only one question.

'And are you a virgin?'

'No,' Alison said, 'but in this vision I've lied for so long, I think I've turned into one.'

That unthinking hand was at the side of her

knee. She could taste his breath and they were still talking and not going anywhere.

'Why would you lie?'

'It's just easier to with my mum.' And it was impossible to explain, so she didn't try to—impossible to tell this gorgeous, free man about the tentacles that were tightening ever more firmly around her, impossible to admit what he could never understand.

'Do you get them?' She broke the silence.

'What?'

'Visions of a possible future.'

'No.' His mouth found her cheek and then slid to her ear and she was terribly glad she'd cleaned them.

'Never?' Alison checked, trying to talk, trying to breathe, trying very hard not to kiss him. 'Don't you see scenarios, like if you don't do this, then that might happen?'

He nibbled at her neck while he thought about it. 'At work.' Nick stopped in mid-nibble with his answer. 'Sometimes when I'm looking at an injury I know if we don't do that or prescribe that, then this might happen.'

He got it.

'And in your life?' Alison asked, rolling into him, feeling his jean-clad sandy legs in between her bare ones, feeling his long, tanned fingers circling her nipples through her T-shirt, and she wanted to rest her breast in his palm, just kissing and lying and talking, and her body was the most alive it had ever been.

'No.' But Nick did think about it as he played with her breasts and what she loved the most was that he *did* think about it. 'Actually, I did have one.' His hands moved from her breasts and made lovely strokes through the cotton on her skirt down her stomach as he spoke. 'When

I was having my supposed premature midlife crisis.' He could see her teeth as she smiled. 'I was on call and the baby was screaming, the nanny had the night off and we were rowing because Gillian was working the next day…' He blinked at his own admission. 'I get it.'

'What was the nanny's name, then?' Alison asked.

'My visions aren't that detailed,' Nick said. 'Helga?' he offered, but she shook her head. 'Svetlana?'

'Better,' Alison said.

And he got it and that came with reward—her lips, unworried, met his and he kissed her mouth and pressed her into the sand. She felt the damp salt of the ocean on his shirt and she tasted it on his mouth.

She felt the press of his leg and the roam of his hands, the sand in her hair and the slide of his tongue, and the dangerous beckoning of his loaned flat, and the pull of her home, all tightening in her stomach as his mouth pursued.

It was a kiss that struck at midnight, and she turned, but only in his arms, a kiss that had her hips rise into his groin, and it could never be enough.

A kiss that had her breast slip out of her bra and though encased in fabric still fall into his palm.

A kiss where you didn't have to go further to enjoy it, but for Alison it was already too late to stay, though it was Nick who pulled away, because if he kissed her for a moment longer, he would forget they were on a beach!

'I ought to go,' Alison said.

'Yes, you ought to,' Nick said, and she let him help her up, and then he did the nicest of things—he dusted her down.

It was *the* nicest thing.

The stroke of his hand on her body, the attention to detail, the warmth of his palm stroking her bottom and then dusting damp sand from her calves. It was so seemingly innocent but it was like sex with clothes on—actually far better than any sex Alison had ever had—and she stood, compliant, but she wanted to run with him, back to his flat, and never mind the coffee. And she nearly said 'Your turn', nearly put her hands out to deal with his sandy jeans, but he took her hand instead because it would have been far too dangerous, and they walked up the beach, tossed the bottle in the bin and then headed for her street. They walked in silence to her turn-off and this time when she went to say goodbye, Nick insisted on walking her to her door.

With their kiss she was a little more his, even if just for a little while, which meant he walked with her. She just wished he wouldn't, but couldn't say so.

'We're both off at the weekend.' Nick knew because he'd looked. 'I was thinking of getting a bike, going for a ride in the mountains…' He sensed her reluctance and misinterpreted it. 'I'll book two rooms.'

'I don't know, Nick.' So badly she wanted to go, but it wasn't just the weekend and sleeping arrangements that had her in knots, but getting on a bike, the recklessness of it—all of it. 'Actually, I've got some things I need to do and then I've got a week of nights…' And the evening ended there, and she gave him just a little kiss on the cheek, because she knew her mother was watching, and she knew too that he was watching her as she walked to her door.

He was.

And he must be getting good at her vision game, because as Nick walked home he was having one of his own and there wasn't a crying baby or Svetlana in sight, more an Alison uncut vision.

Alison let loose, Nick thought with a smile, pulling up in surprise at just how much he wanted to share his vision with her…

'Oh, you're back.' Rose stood by the kettle, as if she hadn't been at the window. 'I was just making a cup of tea to take back to bed. Do you want one?'

'No, thanks, Mum.'

'Nice night.'

'Really nice.'

'How was your friend?'

'Great,' Alison said, hearing the singular, and she turned to go to bed, but then relented. 'We just had some pasta, and then walked.'

'You're covered in sand.'

'We walked on the beach.'

Rose humphed, and no doubt there was half the beach in her hair and why did she feel guilty? Why was her mother sulking when she had done absolutely nothing wrong? 'Am I allowed to ask his name?'

Alison hesitated. It was all too new and too soon to be naming him, she wanted to pull apart her own thoughts and feelings without sharing things first, but her mum wanted conversation, inclusion, and at every turn Alison did try.

'Nick,' Alison said, and her mum just waited. 'He's a friend from work. So what did you do tonight?'

'Not much—I looked through some photos.' She gave a wan smile. 'I'll have to find something to do once you're gone.'

'I'll be ten minutes away, Mum.'

'Oh.' Rose suddenly changed the subject. 'Your uncle Ken rang. They're having a barbecue at the weekend, so don't go making any plans—they're looking forward to seeing you.'

'What day?' Alison asked, sure, quite sure what was coming next.

'I'm not sure…' Rose's forehead crinkled as she tried to recall. 'Memory like a sieve—I'll ring tomorrow.'

To arrange a sudden barbecue, Alison thought, but didn't say. ''Night, Mum.' She kissed her mother on the cheek and went upstairs, headed for her room and wished, wished, wished she'd met Nick in a couple of months' time, when she had her own flat.

But as Alison climbed into bed, she knew it wasn't that simple.

In thirty days' time, twenty-eight, in fact, she'd have been in more of a position to let him into her life.

To climb on a bike and head into the hills and,

yes, maybe not tonight, but the way her body had thrummed to his kiss, soon, very soon, the night would have had a very different conclusion. Her own reaction tonight, though so natural at the time, startled her now as she lay there. She wanted to ring him, right now this minute, to explain that this was out of character for her. That wine and kisses on the beach… She burnt at the memory, but it was in embarrassment now. She wasn't like that—well, she was, but only with him.

He'd hardly appreciate the admission, Alison realised. Nick had wanted fun, so too had she.

Maybe it was better this way, Alison decided, turning to the wall and willing sleep to come.

Maybe caution was merited here, even if she resisted it, because, as a little voice in her head grew louder, Nick would be around for a couple of months only and two weeks of that had already gone.

Yes, if she had the flat, if she had some freedom, she could let him more into her life.

But how much harder would it be then to have him leave?

CHAPTER SEVEN

'ALISON, could I have a word?' Nick caught her right at the end of her shift on Friday when all week she'd done her absolute best to avoid him.

Of course they'd talked, but about patients and things, and Alison had been very careful to take her break only when Nick was busy with a patient, but just as she thought she'd got through the working week he caught her at three-twenty p.m. as she and Ellie headed for the bus stop.

'I'm rushing for the bus.'

'We've already missed it, the next one isn't due for twenty minutes.' Ellie, dear Ellie, beamed. 'I'll wait for you at the stop.'

'Sorry,' he started, 'I haven't been avoiding

you, and there just hasn't been a chance to talk to you.'

'I know.' Alison smiled, even though she'd engineered it that way. 'It's been a crazy week.'

'Look, about this weekend,' Nick said. 'I thought we could go out.'

'You're going away.'

'I'd rather…' There was a rare awkwardness to him. 'I'm happy to give it a miss. I'd rather spend some time with you.'

'I've got a family thing tonight…' Alison said, which was now true. 'My dad's brother's having a barbecue, it's always a bit awkward…' She saw him frown. 'My dad's dead, we get together and it always ends up a bit of a reminisce…'

'What about the rest of the weekend?' Nick was direct. It was a barbecue she was going to after all, so she struggled for an answer, one that let her off the hook.

'I really have to go to the home furnishings

store.' It was the most pathetic of excuses. 'I need some stuff for the flat.'

Somehow, and she really didn't know how and certainly not why, but for reasons of his own, a shopping trip and dinner at his place afterwards was more appealing to Nick than a bike ride in the mountains and somehow, and she did know why, he was still so very easy to talk to, still so very hard not to want to like. 'I need to give the car a run,' Nick explained when he offered to pick her up, 'or the battery will go flat.'

'I'll see.' She gave him a thin smile. 'I just need to…' She didn't bother to explain, in fact she didn't have to explain, Alison realised, didn't have to tell him about every beat of her heart. 'I'll let you know.'

She caught up with Ellie at the bus stop. 'Thanks a lot.' Alison gave her friend a wry smile. 'I was actually trying to get away back there!'

'Then you're mad!' Ellie said. 'He's gorgeous, he's nice and from the way he's always looking at you or, oh, so casually asks "Who's on a late today?" or "Who's on in the morning?" and loses interest after it gets to your name, I think we can all safely assume he likes you. Lucky thing.'

'Hardly—he's only here for a few weeks.'

'So?' Ellie gave her an odd look.

'There's just no point.'

'Well, I suppose there's no point if you're looking for a husband.' Ellie let out a laugh. 'I don't get you, Alison. He's gorgeous. You were saying the other week you wanted some fun and adventure, and now it's handed to you on a plate…'

She wished, how she wished she could be more like Ellie, could see only the positives, but all Alison could see was a sure-fire recipe for hurt and she told Ellie so.

'I like him,' she admitted. 'I could see myself *really* liking him.'

'So go for it.'

'You know what Mum's like,' Alison said. 'Once I've got my own place…'

Ellie just laughed. 'How did you survive your teens? I mean, before…' Yes, Ellie laughed at most things, but her voice did trail off then. She genuinely liked Rose and knew all Alison had been through.

'Tim was the one who was always in trouble.' Alison could smile at the memory now. 'I used to just say I was staying at a friend's if I wanted to go out.'

'Do that, then.' Ellie shrugged. 'Till you get your own place, say you're staying at mine. Anyway, by then you might find out that he's the most crushing bore, or walk in to find him dressed in your underwear and stilettos. Go out and have some fun, for God's sake…he doesn't have to be "the one" to enjoy him.'

Ellie was right.

Alison stepped off the bus and instead of heading for home she walked on the beach, sensible shoes in hand. She felt the sand between her toes, and the sun warming her back, tasted the salt on her lips and felt the wind in her hair, and for the first time in years she tasted adventure, for the first time in so long Alison felt just a little bit free.

She'd yearned for adventure, escape, and Nick was just that.

Nick didn't need to know all of her—Nick didn't need to know that the nights out and kisses on the beach were rarities.

She could do this, Alison told herself, walking past the very spot where they had lain. She could throw caution to the wind, could be the woman her body was begging her to be, could close her mind to the pitfalls and problems and for once just enjoy.

But how? the sensible part of her mind asked. When even staying out after midnight required the stealth and ability to lie like a teenager to her mum. Surely the last thing Nick needed from a holiday romance was the crush of her problems landing in his lap.

Why should she put herself through it?

Because you want to.

Nick's voice seemed to carry on the wind, echoing her own thoughts, and she *did* want to.

And surely she could handle it?

She was far too serious about things, Alison conceded. It didn't have to be for ever to be worthwhile.

Around 10:30 if you can still make it.

She held her breath and sent the text and then held it again till he replied: *Great.*

And Ellie was right again.

She didn't want to lie to her mum, she didn't want to *have* to lie to her mum, but she did enjoy having him in her life.

And he could never be boring. As for Ellie's other suggestion, well, the thought made her laugh.

Right there at the barbecue that evening, as she cut herself a slice of pavlova, she let out a little laugh so, yes, she did enjoy having him in her life, even when he wasn't there.

As she stood, chatting to her uncles and aunts, there was an inner glow in knowing that she would see him tomorrow, just this extra smile as she described the flat to her uncle Ken, because she'd seen it with Nick.

'I'm going to look at furniture tomorrow,' Alison said as her mum came over. 'I want to look at desks.'

'I might come along,' Rose replied. 'I was

thinking of getting some bar stools for the kitchen bench. Are you taking Tim's car?'

It was one of the reasons she rarely drove; the car would always be Tim's. Her mother wouldn't part with it, insisted Alison use it, then got teary when she did.

'Actually, Nick's taking me.'

'Nick?' Ken smiled, pleased to see his favourite niece not just with a sparkle in her eyes but gently standing up to his sister-in-law.

'A friend from work,' Alison said, smiling back at her uncle.

And friends dropped around and friends were asked in.

'Mum, this is Nick.'

Alison tried very hard to treat him as if it were Ellie or Moira or just any friend coming in on Saturday morning before they headed out for a shopping expedition. Rose did the same as

Alison finished getting ready, offering him a cup of tea, which Nick accepted, and chatting to him about the hospital and about England and how she and her late husband had wanted to take a trip around Europe when they retired.

'So you're just here for a couple of months, then?' Alison heard her mum saying as she walked into the kitchen.

'That's the plan.' Nick nodded. 'I've got a cousin in New Zealand who's getting married.' Nick was pleasant and polite, and from the way he chatted he was in no rush to head out—in fact, he even accepted Rose's offer of some toast and ginger marmalade.

'Alison can't stand it,' Rose said as Alison rolled her eyes. 'It was Tim's favourite.'

'Tim?' Nick said as the air in Alison's chest stopped moving.

'My son,' Rose said, and thankfully Nick didn't push. But his eyes swept past her a couple of times to the endless photos on the mantelpiece and when Alison went to her bedroom to find a missing shoe, it came as no surprise when Rose followed her.

'What time will you be back from the shops?'

'Actually…' Alison swallowed. 'There's a party on tonight. Vicky, one of the A and E nurses, is getting engaged.' She saw her mother's rapid blink. 'I told you last week.' Which she had, and it was true, except Vicky was actually Ellie's friend and Alison's was more a casual invitation than an expected guest, and she could have sworn she felt her nose grow a touch as she continued. 'She's down the road from Ellie—Ellie said I could stay at hers.' She gave her mum a hurried kiss on the cheek. 'I'll text and let you know what's happening.'

And then finally, *finally*, they were in the car and heading off, and following blue lines to a parking spot.

'You'd rather this than a bike ride in the mountains?' Alison commented as she grabbed a pencil and tape measure.

'We can do that another time,' Nick replied, and Alison walked on in silence. 'I've missed this.' He nudged her as they walked through. 'I'm not joking. I want to do something *normal*.'

He was actually very helpful. The fact he had seen the flat, combined with a male brain, meant he could remember strange details like there was a window where she wanted *that* large bookshelf, and that there was no way on earth that desk was going to fit where Alison intended.

'It's the same the world over.' Nick grinned as they sat in the canteen with their meatballs and chips and red berry jam amidst frazzled couples, yet maybe because they weren't a couple and it wasn't *their* bed or their sofa they were buying, they could just sit there and enjoy. Nick even bought her a little bottle of wine with a glass that screwed to the bottle.

'I'm going to keep this.' Alison was delighted.

'Emergency supplies for your bedroom!' Nick said, and went up to get one for himself too. It was just a tiny reference that he'd picked up on the tension at home, though he said nothing else about it.

Not until later, much later when they were sitting on the balcony, having eaten a mountain of prawns. Nick had cooked and Alison had tossed a salad—a ten-minute meal that would stay in her memory for ever. They were looking out at the ocean and the view was somehow nicer than the one from the bus and from the one walking on the beach. The sun was setting behind them, the colours reflecting on the water, and the waves were very active that evening. She had pinched one of his jumpers and it was worrying how nice his company was, how thrilling it felt to just be with him—for normal things to be so invigorating. He made no suggestion that they go out, or head off to Vicky's party, gave no indication the day had been less exciting than what he was used to.

In fact, for Nick, silence, mutual silence, was lovely.

For months now he'd been a guest—in another country, or at a friend's, or a hotel or hostel, or a hospital—with strangers who were about to become friends. Yes, it was fun and exhilarating, but it was also exhausting—perpetual new faces at breakfast, having to dress for bed in case you needed to get up in the night to go to the loo. It had been a welcome relief to have, after all this time, a flat to himself and a glimmer of a routine, but he shared that precious space with surprising ease now.

And looking over at Alison, who was staring out to the ocean she loved, there was no need to regale, just a deeper need to know, to go that bit further, to find out a little more, and so he asked her.

'What happened to Tim?'

She'd sort of known that the question would come all day, and in some way she'd been waiting for it.

'He was with my dad,' Alison said. 'They were fishing.' He didn't say anything and she was glad of that. 'The weather wasn't that bad, probably a day like this. They got into trouble, ended up too close to the rocks…'

'When?'

'Two, nearly three years ago. I'd finished my training—I was doing some shifts in emergency before I headed off overseas.'

'They weren't, I mean, you weren't there when they…?' She could hear the dread in his voice and immediately she shook her head.

'No. I wasn't at work or anything. I was sharing a flat with friends. I got a call from Mum to come straight home and the police were at the house when I got there. It was all over by then.'

'Doesn't it kill you,' Nick said, after a very long silence, 'working in Emergency?'

Again Alison shook her head.

'I like it. Dad and Tim never even got to Emergency—at least the people who get there have some chance. It's nice to see that there are some happy endings, despite the most terrible odds.'

'It's not just the kids that upset you, is it?' He remembered that morning how he had learnt something, he just wasn't sure what.

'It's the family.' Alison nodded. 'All that's taken away, and the chaos that they're thrown into...not just the ones who are killed. Like with David. That interview was so important to him—and it all just fell apart. I know in the greater scheme of things his wife and daughter were far more important, but I can remember when Tim and Dad had their accident—I was supposed to be flying out at the weekend and I knew it didn't matter, but it did.' She closed her eyes as she tried to explain it. 'I felt selfish even thinking about me, but I did and I wanted someone to step in, to cancel the tickets, to deal with the airline, to deal with the details, to help look after Mum.'

'How's your mum now?'

Alison shrugged. 'Stuck in a time warp, really. I moved home when it happened, but…' She looked over into his kind green eyes and even though she'd sworn not to land it on him, somehow, under his gaze, she could. 'She's petrified of anything happening to me. I'm petrified of it too,' Alison admitted. 'Not for me, though, but for her. I mean, how would she cope if something happened to me?'

'You can't live like that.'

'I know,' Alison said. 'Which is why in a few

weeks' time I'll have my own place, and won't have to account for my every move.' She gave him a smile, tried to move the conversation away, because he didn't belong in that space. 'It's complicated.' She gave a small shrug. 'It doesn't matter.'

Except it did.

It did matter, because when they were lying on his sofa and revisiting that kiss on the beach, only this time without Alison having her top on, when she should be able to close her eyes and just sink into him, she was all too aware that she was five minutes away from a call that needed to be made—a lie that she was willing to tell.

His back was against the sofa, his long legs holding her from falling, and there was a film coming to end of which they'd only seen the opening credits, and there was the bliss of privacy for them both. His mouth was on her ear and his hand was stroking her breast. Her hands, which had traced his chest, were stealing downwards now. They had left the balcony door open but neither the roar of the ocean nor his kiss in her ear could dull the call of duty. She wriggled back just a little, breathless and moist from his kiss. Yes, hell yes, she would lie for him.

'I've just got to make a phone call.' His mouth was in her neck and her body was in his arms and it was almost torture to pull just a little further away. She didn't know whether to pull on her top and hamper an easy return to his arms, but neither did she want to shiver half-naked in his bathroom.

'And tell her what?' His question came as a surprise, not to Alison but to Nick. He shouldn't ask, he told himself, because it was no business of his, and he shouldn't really care.

He just did.

'Nick?' She shook her head, would not elaborate—was a little cross even as he thwarted her attempts to stop reality invading. 'I won't be a moment.'

'Alison.' He caught her wrist and even though she'd been half-naked in his arms, she felt stupid standing there with her top half exposed, could feel the blush creeping down over her chest as he asked questions a man like Nick shouldn't have to. 'You don't have to lie for me.'

'Who said I'm lying?'

'They did.' He pointed to her rosy breasts and somehow she almost managed a smile.

'My mum's…' Alison swallowed, she truly didn't want to land him with all of it; even Ellie, who had seen it all, struggled to fathom how rigid her mother could be. 'She's difficult.'

'They often are,' Nick said, and he handed her her top. 'And with all she's been through.'

'She was the same before,' Alison admitted,

'though when Dad and Tim were there…' She couldn't really explain, but without further explanation Nick seemed to understand.

'You weren't in the full spotlight?' When she nodded he continued, 'So where are you tonight?'

'Don't worry about it.' She tried blasé, tried casual, but Nick could tell otherwise and she knew it. 'You really picked the wrong girl to have your torrid Sydney fling with.'

And he looked up at her and was silent for a moment because, yes, he had. He could see stains of hurt in her serious brown eyes and he didn't want to add to them, except inevitably he already had. Already this was turning into something else, something bigger, something he hadn't come to Australia for.

'It doesn't feel like a fling,' Nick admitted.

'It's all it can be.' Alison was practical, even if she was shaking inside.

'Come on.' He stood and looked around for his keys. 'I'll walk you home.'

'It's five minutes away.'

And he should say goodnight here, Nick knew. End it here.

But Nick never went for the easy option, so he reached for his keys.

'You're not walking on your own.'

They walked back to Alison's home in pensive silence, and he didn't kiss her on the doorstep, because he knew she didn't want him to, but as she let herself in her mouth still tingled from his and her body held the scent and memory of him. Her eyes must have glittered with stirred passion because Rose's face screamed of martyrdom as she offered Alison a cup of tea. Even though she didn't want tea, even though she wanted to go to bed and think of Nick and read the text he'd just sent because she could feel the vibration of her phone in her bag, that this time made her feel giddy with wanting to read it, she said, 'That would be nice,' and curled up on the sofa and took the mug from her mum.

'I thought you were at a party.'

And instead of saying she had been, or offering the usual half-truth, Alison was honest.

'We gave it a miss,' she admitted. 'We went back to Nick's for dinner.'

'He seems nice,' Rose said, because after all he'd brought her baby home.

'He is nice.'

'How long did he say he was here for?' Skilfully, so skilfully, Rose took the pin and deflated the bubble Alison was floating on. Carefully, lovingly, perhaps, she warned her daughter that this could never, ever be. 'Nice-looking man,' Rose said. 'He must have broken a few hearts on his travels,' she added, just to make sure her daughter got it.

'I'm going to bed.' Alison tried to keep her voice light.

She peeled off her clothes and read her text, which was hardly torrid, hardly from a man hell bent on getting in her knickers and promptly breaking her heart. It just thanked her for a nice day and a really nice night, that he'd enjoyed it.

She should stop this now, common sense said.

Just turn her back on his charm, because there really was no point.

She swam between the flags, certainly wasn't into casual relationships, and that was really all it could be with Nick. In a few weeks he'd be off and she'd be left, and if she wasn't extremely careful, Alison knew she'd be nursing a broken heart.

Actually, she already knew she would be.

He'd arrived in her life as blonde and as dazzling as summer. He just lit everything up and enhanced it all some more.

She didn't get him, but she wanted to.

She wanted the little bit of him that was possible, because there was something about Nick that got her, something that was…just a little bit like the single word she sent back to him.

Same. x

CHAPTER EIGHT

'I'M NOT stalking you!'

She grinned as she walked across the foyer to Emergency on Monday night and Nick joined her. 'Amy asked yesterday if I could cover her week of nights.'

'Oh.'

'I got called in yesterday,' Nick explained.

'I didn't see you on the bus.'

'I drove. It was a last-minute thing. I didn't know whether to ring and offer a lift…' He admitted only a quarter of it—if the truth were told, he hadn't known what to do, full stop.

Despite her kisses, despite the thrum between them, there was more to Alison, of that he was sure. He didn't want to hurt anyone, didn't want to get involved.

Or that was what he had told himself.

Sunday had been spent turning down offers to go out, and not just from colleagues. He'd been called in for a multi-trauma late afternoon and had found a rather blatant card from a Louise H., reminding him where she worked and that she'd love to see him there.

It would actually have been the safer option.

Instead he'd accepted Amy's suggestion they ring out for takeaways, which they'd eaten in her office. The conversation had been easy and before he'd known it, the clock had been edging towards midnight and he'd agreed to take over her week of nights.

But Alison was on nights too.

He headed straight for the staffroom, Alison to her locker, and if she hurried there was time for a drink before she started.

'God!' Moira was tying back her hair. 'I'm tired before we've even started. Try sharing a house with eight travellers and doing a week of night shift!' She gave her dazzling smile. 'All worth it, though.' They walked through to the staffroom and Moira gave a delighted whoop as she saw Nick. 'Are you on nights too?'

''Fraid so.'

'Now, that *does* cheer me up,' Moira said, and she was just so light and uninhibited with her banter, Alison would have killed for a little of the same. 'There's not a spare room at that fancy house of yours, is there?' Moira rattled on. 'For a fellow travelling night worker?'

'It's a one-bedroomed flat.' Nick grinned.

'Move over in the bed, then!' Moira winked. Of course, she had no idea about Alison and Nick, she was just having fun…

Sort of.

'Alison.' Sheila popped her head around the

staffroom door. 'We've had a lot of staff ring in sick tonight. Mary will be in charge, but apart from that it's agency.' She gave a brief smile to Moira and a couple of the others. 'Luckily it's been quiet. The wards all have beds, so you shouldn't have too many problems. Can you make sure the restocking and drug orders get done, and make sure the trolleys are all wiped down. Oh, and there's a list up on the notice-board—you need to do a refresher lifting course. Make sure you tick off what session you're attending.'

So Alison did, and tried not listen to Moira's chatter and Nick's easy replies—tried not to feel as if he was surely thinking he'd set his sights on the wrong girl. After all, he and Moira were both here on holiday.

This was her life.

It showed in so many little ways through out

the night, perhaps because it was a particularly quiet one.

Moira and the other nurses sat chatting when it was quiet.

Alison did the stock ordering. Working around them, she climbed up on footstools to count packets of gauze, and to everyone else Nick appeared not to notice her. He did notice, she knew, because she could feel his lingering eyes at times, or a smile that was there waiting every now and then when she looked up and turned round.

He was brilliant with each and every patient that came through the doors, but during the many, many lulls that filled this quiet night Nick scrolled through his social networking site—there was no registrar's office bulging with a backlog of work for him…probably because there was no backlog when you were just passing through.

'Moira,' Alison asked, 'can you put these boxes away?'

'Sure.' Moira jumped off her stool. 'Where do they go?'

'In the second storage room.'

And she *was* willing, but by the time Alison had shown her where it was, and when for the third time she had to borrow Alison's ID to gain access, it was just far easier to do it herself. There was just a touch of a martyred air to Alison as an hour later she took a gulp of cold tea in the nurses' station and found out all the biscuits she'd brought in were gone.

'I've bought earplugs,' Moira chatted on happily, 'but hopefully everyone will be so hungover, no one will be up before midday and I can get some peace and quiet. I'm a shocking sleeper on nights. What about you, Nick?'

'Sorry?'

'How do you sleep on nights?'

'Like a log,' Nick said, without looking up from the computer, and Alison realised that despite being pleasant, despite the good-natured bantering, there was no flirting from Nick, that he gave nothing back to Moira, as he hadn't to Louise. It was aimed all at her, Alison realised as now he did look up from the computer and gave her a very nice smile, those green eyes turning her pink as she gave a small smile back.

'Is there anything you need me to do?'

'Nothing,' Alison said. It was five a.m., the board was clear and as Nick checked an X-ray with the resident he stretched and yawned. 'I'm going to lie down—call if you need me.'

'Lucky,' Alison grumbled, hauling out the trolleys to be cleaned, and for just a moment their eyes met and Nick felt as if he was back in far North Queensland, standing on a platform with a piece of elastic around his ankle, wanting to jump, knowing it was reckless, ridiculous, that there was no rhyme nor reason to it, yet wanting to all the same.

'What time do you finish?'

'By the time we've given handover—about seven-thirty.'

'I'm here till eight, if you want to hang around—I'll be quicker than the bus.'

He would be, there wasn't one till ten minutes to.

'Thanks,' Alison said.

She cleaned and polished the trolleys, and tried not to think about it as she dealt with the occasional patient, who was seen by the resident and didn't require Nick.

In the morning, when Moira was still teasing for a loan of his bed and he was skilfully deflecting her thinly disguised offer, the rest of the night team, apart from Mary, sped off on the dot of seven-thirty. Alison hung around for a quick chat with Ellie, put her name on the list for the lifting refresher course and then, when Sheila asked if she had five more minutes to go over some annual leave requests, she nodded. When there was nothing else to linger for, except Nick, he walked down the corridor, blonde, tired, offering a lift. Alison smiled and said thanks.

When with him, when it was just them, the doubts that plagued her when they were apart were silenced as always.

'Better than the bus?' Nick asked as she sank back into the passenger seat.

'This morning—yes,' Alison admitted.

'Do you drive?' He glanced over.

'Sometimes—I just prefer the bus for work. The traffic getting in and the staff car-park is impossible sometimes so it's nice just to sit and read the paper.'

'It's been nice *not* driving,' Nick admitted,

'but I can't stand the thought of a bus ride after being on all night—I'd fall asleep.'

'It's always happening to me,' Alison said. 'I end up being woken by the driver.'

He was so easy to talk to—about the complicated, about the mundane—but even though they chatted easily, there was a definite charge in the air, which had a sleepy Alison on the alert. He must have shaved yesterday morning, rather than before coming to work, because he was clearly unshaven now, she noticed. Just as she noticed when he pulled on dark glasses against the glare of the morning sun. Just as she noticed his long tanned fingers tapping on the steering-wheel as they sat in heavy traffic.

'Do you sleep well?' Nick asked, because he had heard about the whole nursing crew's habits and he wanted to find out about hers.

'Depends,' Alison said. 'Mum's at work so the house is quiet…' And her voice trailed off, because somehow that charge in the air intensified, and there was this pause, this silent pondering, a false night that stretched ahead and a shining window of opportunity.

'Do you want to go somewhere for breakfast?' Nick asked as the bay came into view.

'No, thanks,' Alison said, because she wasn't thinking about breakfast.

Just bed.

Bed.

And though they were both tired and sleepy and longing for bed, as he pulled up outside her door, there was no denying it—they were longing for each other too—and as naturally as breathing she turned to him. There was no awkwardness, no will he, won't he, just the bliss of a night spent looking and thinking and pretending you didn't want to, all melting away now that no one else was around. It was a really nice kiss, a slow, morning kiss that could tip easily to more, but there was no way she was asking him in because Alison knew where his kiss could lead and probably there was no chance of her mum coming home, but she just couldn't put herself or her mother in that situation.

'Have a good sleep.' She pulled her mouth away, but she wanted to dive back in.

'I doubt it,' Nick said, and Alison doubted she would either.

She was a kiss away from his bed, Nick knew that, and for the first time in his quest for freedom Nick felt as if he needed to spell out the rules, needed to be very sure that she knew, and so he said it.

He made himself say it.

'I can't stay...'

And she smiled and was very brave, even managed a little joke. 'I didn't ask you in.'

But he wasn't talking about that—she knew

he wasn't talking about that as she climbed out of his car.

He watched her walk up the garden path and for the first time in a long time, at least where women were concerned, Nick was confused—Nick the one almost willing her not to turn round—because of how much he wanted her, and for the foreseeable future, this wasn't how it was supposed to be.

Except this was how it was.

She was exhausted, utterly and completely exhausted, but though her body ached for bed as she walked up her garden path, she ached for him too. It was just criminal that a few streets apart he'd be in bed and she'd be in bed and they had a whole day, a whole wonderful day, if only she would take it. She had her key in the front door, and she opened it, turned round to give him a wave, and he just sat there, looking at her, and she stood there, looking at him, and wished he'd drive off, would just go, except he didn't.

Then she panicked that he would drive off, that he'd pull off the handbrake and she'd miss her chance.

Her one lovely chance to be wild and brave and sexy and impulsive.

Alison slammed the door closed again and turned round. She could see his smile even from the garden, see the want in his eyes as she made the one reckless decision of her life and sped down the garden path. He had the passenger door open before Alison got there. She jumped in like an eager puppy, and he was an equally eager master because he was pulling her in and kissing her, this smothering kiss that sighed and groaned with mutual consent of what was to come. There was just a flicker of sanity, of what would the neighbours think because it was eight a.m. and they were necking like teenagers. Then he pulled back and gave her the most fantastic smile and Alison, who had craved wild, craved passion and adventure, took a breath, took the plunge, and what she said was from her wildest dreams, because she said what Alison Carter would never have—looked into eyes that looked into hers, and in the mirror of them she saw herself, found herself, was finally herself. 'I want breakfast in bed.'

CHAPTER NINE

HE KISSED her even as the front door closed and for a moment, just a moment, she did wonder what the hell she was doing and tried not to worry that she'd been working all night and must smell of hospitals, consoling herself, that so too must he, but then his kiss did its magic, produced an Alison that only he could.

'You taste fantastic.' She said her thoughts out loud, because with him she could, and his hands roamed her body, as they had been longing to all night, and she leant against the hall wall and he kissed her some more.

It was a relief to get to the bedroom.

Yes, it had the most stunning view from the bedroom, except they didn't want to see it. It was an exercise in frustration as they tried to quickly close the blinds and for the first time she heard him swear as it stuck halfway down, but then, yippee, they were closed and he was kissing her again.

'God, Alison…' He made light work of the buttons on her blouse because he'd been undoing them in his head all night. He stripped her—it was such a brilliant word, Alison thought. He stripped her blouse, her navy three-quarter-length Capri pants, he stripped her mind of doubt because his hands and mouth adored her, he stripped her of care and worry till all that was left was her bra and panties and a mind that was free. Now it was her turn and she would, Alison decided as she took off the grey shirt he had been wearing that first day, remember this for ever and ever, because she'd been guessing and peeking and driving herself insane with imagination. Now the big day was here and, unlike Nick, she didn't tear open the wrappers on her parcels. No, she had a nice feel of his chest through the material, tried one more image of what might be inside and slowly, very slowly, tongue on her bottom lip, she peeled one button open, and then another, and he was telling her to hurry but she refused to be rushed.

One more button and she could see a flat brown nipple. She ran her hand over it then bent her head and kissed it, and she could feel his hands undoing her bra, feel the drop of aching breasts as he freed her. Yet still she would not be rushed. She had his shirt open a little more now, down to that lovely flat stomach, and all his online pictures combined couldn't capture how nice it was in real life, taut and smooth. She ran her hands over him and he was pulling off her bra and she slid down his shirt and then she went back for another taste of his nipple, heard him moan, felt his hands in her hair and then he moved them, because Nick wanted his pants down.

'Don't spoil my fun.' She pushed his hands away and she was cruel and she wasn't kind. She fiddled with the button and refused to let him help her. He was breathing so hard, his hands toying with her bottom, laid-back Nick, just brimming now with urgency, but she was in no rush.

Well, maybe a little bit, because beneath linen pants that he almost fell over to step out of were the sexiest hipsters and she felt him again, gave her present a little squeeze to gauge it and she couldn't tease any more, because she wanted to see, she wanted to feel, wanted what was hers. And he was completely spectacular, and hers for now and she held it, over and over she held it, till her breathing was doing strange things now, because he had his hands on the cheeks of her bottom and was pressing her into him, and his mouth was on hers and then he wanted more, more of her than he should sensibly want, because when he should be diving in he was diving down, pushing her on the bed and running his mouth up her thighs, and it was Nick in no rush now.

He kissed and he teased and he relished her throb in his mouth, but there was this strange moment, a warning almost, because though it felt like sex and tasted of it too, it was teetering into something more. A place where he had to *remember* to stop, to put on a condom, not just slide up and slide in as he so badly wanted to. A different place, because as he drove deep within her, why was he saying her name over and over?

And this was what he did, Alison reminded herself as she tried to hold back, tried and failed to cling onto that last bit of restraint.

This was what that smile promised, Alison

told herself, except her body didn't want to register dire warnings, it wanted to be free, and trapped beneath him, finally she was.

'It's the quiet ones you have to worry about.' She lay next to Nick and smiled at his voice as she came back to earth and when half an hour later, still neither were sleeping, she said yes when he offered to make a drink and lay there, just a little awkward as to what he was thinking as she heard him walk out to the kitchen.

What *was* he thinking?

Nick wasn't sure as he filled a glass with water and emptied it in one and then, rather than think, he flicked on the television as he waited for the kettle to boil. But there was no solace there, an armchair psychologist was telling him to face up to feelings, to be honest with himself—only Nick didn't want to.

'How many sugars?' he called down the hall,

because *that* was how it should be, except he remembered before she even answered.

'Have you got any sweeteners?'

He didn't, so she settled for sugar then grumbled that it tasted different as he climbed in bed beside her, then admitted, as Nick lay there, that she actually preferred the real thing.

'It's bad for you, though,' Nick said, and he'd forgotten to turn the television off, so he padded back out and aimed the remote like a loaded gun, because honesty was not the best policy here.

It wasn't just Alison he was worried about hurting here.

It was himself.

CHAPTER TEN

SHE could tell it was Tuesday the second she stepped inside. The slow cooker was on and the scent of beef stroganoff filled the house. Her heart was in her mouth as she waited for her mum to appear and say she'd been off sick and where the hell had she been all day, but the house was still and silent. Alison checked her mobile and the house phone and there were no messages, and *starving* Alison had some stroganoff between two slices of bread and butter then showered and headed straight to bed, to cram in a couple more hours' sleep, which she managed amazingly well. She was woken at six-thirty by her mum's knock on the door.

'Did you sleep well?'

'Really well,' Alison said, hiding her guilty blush.

'Good. I tried not to wake you when I came in. Dinner's almost ready.'

'How was work?' Alison asked as they sat and ate dinner. It was a nice dinner and a nice conversation and they even had a laugh. Alison would miss this and did love her so, it was just the little things that added up, like Nick wanting the crossword and Paul's garlic bread, that built and built until they became big things and change really was needed, because a row with her mother, hurting her mother, Alison would avoid at all costs.

Little things like Rose insisting she take leftovers for her meal break.

'I can put some in a container and you can have it on your break,' Rose offered.

'Put it in the freezer,' Alison said. 'I think I'll get something from the canteen.'

'From the vending machine?' Rose said.

'They do sandwiches and things and there are nice vol-au-vents.'

'Why would you pay for something when you can take it in?' Rose said, pulling out a container and filling it with Tuesday's beef stroganoff.

'I just fancy—'

'You need to be more careful—you've got a mortgage to think of now.'

She took the stroganoff.

Still, it *was* appreciated.

By Nick, who was sick of canteen sandwiches and mushroom vol-au-vents.

To describe a busy week of night shifts as the best week of her life would have once been laughable, but for the first time since the tragedy Alison actually glimpsed normality in upside-down week.

A gorgeous normality where work was busy, a happy normality where she ate dinner with her mum each night and packed leftover dinner for her evening break.

An easy normality, where she didn't have to lie, well, not outright, and she didn't have to race home at midnight. All she had to do was be.

Nick would drive her home. More often than not she'd see her mum at the bus stop or pop in just to check that she had gone, and, just to be sure, Alison would leave a little note on the kitchen bench that read something like, *Gone shopping*, or *At dentist*, which she'd tear up when she got home at four. Then she'd grab some clothes and race down the street to Nick's car, to him, to a gorgeous normality, where they shut the blinds on the world and lay in bed and talked and laughed, and made lovely love, or rather, she corrected herself, had torrid, wild sex and slept.

She knew from the start, though, that it couldn't last.

'Can I borrow you before you go, Nick?' Amy clipped in for her day shift at the end of the week, all scented, suited and gorgeous, as an exhausted Alison subtly hung back for her lift.

'I shouldn't be long,' Nick managed as he disappeared into his colleague's office, but no matter how many times Alison checked the staff roster, and no matter how chatty her colleagues were, by eight-fifteen she was starting to look as if she had no home to go to.

'Where is Amy?' Sheila barked from a cubicle, then marched out to the intercom. 'It's all very well swapping her shifts, but the occasional appearance on the shop floor would be nice.' Her voice was a lot sweeter when she pressed the button. 'Amy, we need you out here.'

'Is it urgent?' came Nick's voice, and Sheila rolled her eyes.

'Pressing, not urgent.'

'Let us know if that changes,' came Nick's firm reply.

'Good luck!' Alison smiled to Sheila as she heaved up her bag and headed for the bus stop, but despite a rapid run she missed it and despite the sun she shivered at the stop, tired and, as Nick's car pulled up a full twenty minutes later, just a little fed up.

'Sorry about that.'

It would have been childish not to get in.

'I was thinking…' Nick negotiated the early-morning traffic easily, even laughed when she grumbled about rush-hour, telling her she should try driving where he lived in England if she wanted a *real* rush-hour, and then he got back to thinking. 'How about we do the Sydney Harbour Bridge climb this weekend?'

'I can't even think about bridges and climbing at this hour.'

'It will be fun.'

Alison could think of other words to describe it and her eyes flicked to the clock on the dashboard—had she left on time and taken the bus, she'd already be in bed. 'What did Amy want?' It was a childish question to ask perhaps, or perhaps it was the edge to her voice, because Nick glanced over.

'There was something she needed to discuss.'

Which gave her no answer and the silence wasn't comfortable as he stopped at the traffic lights and again he looked over at her.

'Don't ask me to betray a confidence, Alison, just because we're…' His eyes shuttered for a moment, perhaps ruing his near choice of words. 'Work's separate,' Nick said. 'We both agreed.'

It wasn't a row, it wasn't anything she could pin down, yet stupidly she felt like crying, relieved almost when Nick stopped at a corner shop and got out. 'I need milk.'

And it was a tiny time out, a welcome time out, because by the time he came out of the shop, all gorgeous and yawning, Alison had convinced herself she was tired, that was all, not questioning and jealous, just ratty, premenstrual and coming off a full week of sex and nights.

'Here.' He handed her one of two newspapers he had bought, gave her a kiss and then smiled. 'There's always a simple solution.'

There just wasn't to this.

And even if they were talking, even if there hadn't been a row, things felt different this morning.

Nick had a call from his boss in the UK then another from his mum, both reminding Alison there was a world that was waiting for him to rejoin it, and she was all too aware that next week she'd be back on days, which meant home by midnight, that the slice of freedom she'd carved for them was drawing to a close and it was either lie there and cry or just pretend to be asleep when a long hour later, damp from the shower, his tired body slipped into bed.

'Alison?' She heard his voice and didn't answer, lay with her eyes closed till she didn't have to pretend any more, didn't have to pretend that she could do this, but it was a fitful sleep, an uneasy sleep. She woke at two, and looked over at him and he really was exquisite.

Alison didn't generally prefer blonds—she just preferred Nick.

He must have felt her wake, because he stirred a bit beside her, rolled a little toward her and his legs trapped hers and pulled her in a bit so her face was closer to his chest. She'd been enjoying looking, but now she was enjoying feeling the sleepy body beside hers as she lay awake, exploring the sensation of his long limbs loosely wrapped around hers and the scent of him. There was more than just thought there, because it woke him, this energy, this want that hauled him from slumber, because he slid her up a little till their faces met.

'Morning.'

'Morning,' Alison answered, even if it was mid-afternoon and, better than a kiss, he answered what was still on her mind.

'Amy was offering me more work.'

'Overtime?'

'Extra time,' Nick said. 'She was just sounding me out, there's nothing definite…'

'Isn't Cort coming back?' Alison blinked, curious for other reasons. Cort had taken leave suddenly three months ago, and all the senior staff had been tight-lipped as to why—as Nick was being now.

'It's not that.' He closed his eyes. 'You can't say anything.'

'I wouldn't.' But Nick wouldn't reveal any

more. Still, that he was considering staying was what she wanted to hear, but she knew his struggle, because hers was the same. 'What about Asia?'

'I can't do both.'

'Could you, though?' Alison asked. 'Could you take more time off?'

'They very reluctantly gave me this year.' It was too much to think about, too much to consider, so he pulled her closer instead and there were forty-seven minutes, give or take, till she had to up and leave, and they both smiled at that pleasurable thought.

Both awake, and even if their minds were racing with new possibilities, their bodies were still pliant and just a little lazy, because they moved in just a little closer, and his legs wrapped around hers a little tighter. The bed was so warm and it felt so nice, and Alison gladly kissed him back, which was so much better than thinking about Asia and careers and sky-high bridges, except the thoughts were in the bed with them too, because it wasn't fair, Alison thought, as his kiss deepened. It wasn't bloody fair, his mouth agreed as he pulled her in tighter. A little lazy, a little bit angry, a little bit reckless, or just greedy for a little bit more. When he pulled her even closer, Alison didn't move back, or away. She could feel his warm, heavy length between her legs, and she wanted him there, and he wanted to be there, because there he stayed a while.

She felt a low tremble in her body as he ran his tip over her moist place, she could feel his kiss deepen even more, feel the tightening of her throat and the flood of desire that bade him on, not consciously, more naturally, just a deepening kiss at both ends of their bodies, and he was just a little way in and her body willed him to go further, beat for him to join her. But sense hauled them back from that dangerous place, Nick rolling over and sheathing himself, Alison dizzy at what they had almost done but grateful for common sense prevailing. Then he was back and, yes, they were both angry, not with the other but at time that wouldn't pause. With every thrust she counted the days and her hips rose, defiant at the injustice.

She *was* angry.

And he let her be.

He let her be selfish and taste his mouth and his chest for as long as she wanted, he let her tension rise till she thought she might push him off, because she didn't know how to feel like this, she didn't know how far she could go. So he showed her, he pushed her, he waited for her, till she stopped counting the days and berating the past, stopped chasing the future till she was in an empty, silent space that was theirs alone to fill—with her scream and his release, with new sensations, deeper sensations than either had felt before.

And something shifted, something definitely shifted, because a little while later, when the alarm bleeped its warning, for the first time Nick grumbled, pulled her back when she said she had to go.

'Stay a bit longer,' Nick said.

And she did.

Alison reset the alarm and climbed back in, wondering if in a few weeks he'd do the same for her.

CHAPTER ELEVEN

LIKE Louise Haversham's toothache, sometimes the agony woke her, but for a while, if she didn't push or probe, Nick's nearing departure was kept at a niggle, a gnawing in the background. Two months had never seemed long enough. In fact, by the time she'd met him, a week of that had already passed, by the time she'd decided to just go for it, another week, and since then she'd seen Sydney thorough the eyes of a tourist, had been on whale-watching trips and a jet-board ride, though she'd declined his suggestion for a tandem sky dive! With the keys to the flat soon to be hers, they were in the final countdown and it wasn't just her feeling it, at every turn she was reminded of the fact. But the hint that

Cort's return might be delayed was her ray of hope on the horizon and Alison was determined to let it shine.

'These are for you!' David said. 'For all of you.' But he smiled especially at Alison as he handed over a large tin of chocolates and he was a different man indeed from the one she had met just a month ago. 'Rebecca's here for her outpatient appointment. We just wanted to stop by and thank everyone.'

'You're more than welcome.' Alison jumped down from her stool and accepted the chocolates. It rarely happened, but when patients came back, it was a treat indeed.

'How's the arm?' Alison asked, and she was thrilled to see Rebecca wiggle all her fingers.

'I'm doing loads of physio, but I'm getting there.' She smiled as Nick and Amy came over and she showed them her moving fingers again.

'I'm glad you're here,' David said to Nick. 'We thought you might be back on your travels.'

'A couple more weeks yet,' Nick said, and Amy rolled her eyes.

'What will we do without you?'

And that niggle was flaring. It was a line Alison was starting to hear far too often when she was around Nick, and it shot an arrow into her heart each and every time she heard it.

'We really are grateful,' David said, and Alison looked at his suit and his smile and the new-found confidence in this family and knew what was coming. 'I got that job, by the way.'

'Fantastic.' She could not have been more pleased. 'That's marvellous.' She was delighted for them all.

'Hello, there!' Ellie joined them and chatted for a moment. 'Has it really been a month?'

And it had been and it was, because just a

couple of days later Alison had a mortgage and a set of keys.

'I don't remember the carpet being *this* green.' She walked around with Nick and wondered if she'd bought the same place. 'Were the walls really brown?'

'It will look great with furniture.' Nick was optimistic and then realistic. 'And a coat of paint.' He saw her glance up at the grey ceiling and then blow her fringe skywards at the job ahead. 'I'll help you. We can go and look at paint this evening and get it done over the next few days.'

'You've got better things to do than paint a flat,' Alison pointed out.

'No.' He pulled her towards him. 'I like spending time with you—here.' He pulled out a present from the bag he had been carrying that had had Alison wondering, and she opened it and it was a plant in a bright red pot that he put on the tiny balcony table. 'That's the garden sorted.'

Then he pulled out champagne and, of course, he'd forgotten glasses, but as they had that night on the beach they sat on the floor and drank from the bottle. Though it was cool and fizzy, Alison just had a mouthful because, yes, the flat was hers and Nick was here and it was a great day, but somehow she was finding it hard to feel like celebrating, especially when Nick pointed out she should hold off getting her furniture delivered till the flat had been painted. It was practical, sensible of course, but she wanted to move in so badly.

'We'll get it done in a week,' Nick said. 'Then we've still got…' His voice trailed off, because then all they would have was a week.

And it just got ever closer—the future was fast approaching and it caught up at six p.m. on the Friday. Alison was trying to wrestle damp legs into her stockings as her mum chatted to Nick in the lounge.

There was a seafood restaurant at the Quay Nick wanted to try and even if it was supposed to be gorgeous and the views and food to die for, Alison was exhausted and, frankly, a box of noodles and a DVD would have sufficed.

She peered at her slightly pale reflection and added a dash more blusher. She could hear the laughter from the living room, because even Rose seemed to have loosened up and was getting on with Nick. Everyone did. It just made it harder, that was all.

'Ready!' She was wearing high heels and a black dress with a sheer black blouse over it, and her hair was behaving. Nick's eyes lit up in pleasure as she walked in and Alison's did the same.

He was in dark trousers and a dark shirt, which accentuated his blondness. She wished her flat was ready and he had picked her up from there!

'What time's the table booked for?' Rose asked.

'Seven,' Nick said, 'so we'd better get a move on.' He kissed Alison on the cheek and he was clearly thinking along the same lines as she was because as Rose turned her attention to the television, he whispered the real time in her ear. 'Eight,' he said, and that made her smile. They were just about to dash off for their supposed seven p.m. booking, but really his flat, when his phone rang. He glanced at it, about to ignore it, then frowned. 'I'd better get this.'

Alison sorted out her bag and checked for lipstick and things as Nick went out to the little garden, and she could hear the restrained delight in his voice, hear him laugh, hear him talk. 'It's a huge surprise!' she heard him say. 'Thanks so much for considering me.' She glanced over at her mum and forced a smile, then poured herself a glass of water as Nick spoke for a little while longer and then came in.

'Work,' Nick said, and Alison gave a tiny frown.

'In England.'

'Oh.'

Rose suddenly remembered she had the iron on in the laundry and Nick must have remembered that he oughtn't to smile quite so widely, because he contained his delight just a touch. 'They've asked me to cut short my trip. Not this bit,' he added hastily, 'just get back from Asia a month early.' As she listened she found out that one of his seniors was leaving and there was a fast track to consultant, and she did absolutely everything right. Alison smiled and kissed him and offered congratulations, but it was the strangest feeling, because she was wishing him well for a time that didn't involve her.

'I haven't said yes,' Nick pointed out.

'It's still something to celebrate—so it's my turn to get the champagne!' Alison said, and she kissed him. She really tried, she did everything right, but Nick couldn't help but compare it to the more genuinely happy response she'd had to David's news, and it didn't irk him.

He got it.

Somehow they didn't dash back to his place for some alone time. Instead, by unvoiced mutual consent, they headed straight to Darling Harbour, walked around for half an hour and then shared a meal that should have been sumptuous, but there was just this sadness in the air and it was Nick who broached it.

'It's not looking hopeful for Asia.'

Alison forced a tight smile. 'You've got offers all round. What's happening with Cort?'

'Cort?' Nick frowned.

'Amy said there might be a spot…'

'That's still up in the air.

'It's going to be harder than I thought.' He took her hand, but it stayed in a ball beneath his. 'Saying goodbye.'

'It's going to be exactly as hard as I thought,' Alison said, and her eyes flashed with tears for the very first time.

'It doesn't have to end just because—'

'Oh, please…' She was almost accusing. 'I'll accept your friendship on Facebook.' Then she shook her head, because she wouldn't.

Because she could not stand the thought of following him, reading about him, and not having him. That at some point she'd have to block him, because he was taking with him her heart.

'We can still keep things going…' But he didn't push it, he paid the bill and though there was conversation, both were hurting.

'Alison,' Nick said as he pulled up at her

house, neither having even suggested they go to his place for a while. 'I never intended… I mean…'

'Why couldn't you have been boring?' Alison turned to him. 'Why couldn't I have found you in high heels and my underwear?' And she started to laugh, but it was squeezed out with tears and Nick pulled her into him and held her for a moment.

'I'll pick you up tomorrow, we'll talk, we'll try and work something out.' His mind raced for solutions, and there was but one he could think of and that required deeper thought. 'Tomorrow,' Nick said, 'I'll pick you up.'

'I don't want to paint.'

'We're not going to paint,' Nick said. 'We're going to work something out. You just be ready at ten.'

'For what?'

'Eight letters,' Nick smiled. 'Starts with S, ends with E.'

'I hate surprises.'

He cupped her face with his hand and looked over to her, as if reading her for the very first time. 'You really do, don't you?'

And she pulled away, stepped out of the car and headed into her house—just a touch shaken by what he'd said, a touch unsure what he'd meant.

A touch worried that he'd stepped on a truth.

CHAPTER TWELVE

'HI, MUM.' She was tired and confused and all Alison wanted was bed, but Rose seemed determined to chat.

'How was it?'

'Lovely,' Alison said.

'You're early.'

'I'm just tired.'

'You didn't go for a walk afterwards?' Rose asked. 'Or back to his place for coffee?'

'I told you…' Alison frowned, unsure what Rose was getting at, but she found out a split second later when her mother's hand slapped her cheek, and furious words erupted from her.

'You tell me nothing!' Rose snarled, and then she tossed a handful of little packages at Alison, like confetti to a bride. 'Strawberry flavoured…' Rose sneered. 'Banana flavoured—you tart!'

'Mum, please…' Shamed, embarrassed, shocked, still she tried to calm things down, but Rose would not let her speak.

'How could you, Alison?'

'I'm twenty-four!' She spelt it out, repeated it, said it again, but Rose would not relent.

'How could you?'

She was seventeen again, only there wasn't her dad or Tim to deflect her mother. It was ridiculous and they both knew it—and for the first time Alison told her mother so.

'You turned a blind eye with Paul.'

'Paul was serious about you!' came Rose's savage reply.

'So's Nick. He's not using me.' Alison's voice was rising, but she wasn't just arguing with Rose, she was arguing with herself. 'It's not some fling…'

'It's exactly what it is,' Rose responded. 'What? Do you think he's going to give it all up? You heard him tonight. He's got a promotion. It couldn't possibly work. And you're *sleeping* with him.' It was all too close to the bone for Alison and she sat there and tried to take it, but Rose would not stop. 'You were always trouble, always the one we worried about, always wild, and yet it was poor…' She stopped, but not in time. The words might just as well have been said—Alison had lived, Tim had died. It stung and it burnt and tears shot from her eyes, not just at her mother's thoughts but what she had done to her brother's memory.

'Tim was fun, Tim knew how to laugh. You've canonised him, Mum, you've turned him into some sort of saint. No matter what I do, I can never live up to him.'

'Alison…' Rose maybe realised she had

gone too far. 'This isn't about Tim, it's about this man.'

'This man,' Alison said, 'is called Nick, and he makes me laugh and he makes me happy. And…' she threw the condoms on the floor '…you have no right to go through my things. I can't wait to move out!' In fact, she didn't have to wait now. 'I'm going.'

'With him?'

And Rose broke down then, just melted onto the chair. And Alison wanted to storm out, to go to bed, to curl up in a ball, but instead she sat with her arms around her mum, her own tears not helping her stinging cheek. Yes, it was a row that had needed to be had, but Alison knew what it was really all about.

'I was talking about the flat. I'm not going to England, Mum.' She stroked her mum's shoulders. 'He's not going to ask, and if by some miracle he did, I wouldn't go.'

She wouldn't.

She couldn't.

She'd had it confirmed now.

It wasn't about Nick, it wasn't about England. It could be Thailand, or a bungee jump, or a car, or a wave, and the row would have been the same. Even if cruel words had been spoken, she knew she was loved—it just stifled her.

'I'm not going to England,' Alison repeated. 'I may be moving into a flat, but I'm not going to leave you—I never would, Mum. But—' she was firm, really firm with her mum for the first time '—I do have to live.'

CHAPTER THIRTEEN

IT WAS horribly awkward the next morning.

'Yes, please' to tea, and 'No, thanks' to toast.

And 'You should eat something.'

'I'm honestly not hungry.' Alison wasn't—she felt sick when she thought of the condoms, and just all churned up from their row. She had no idea what was happening today either. She had a bikini on beneath her denim skirt and halter neck and something a little more dressy laid out on her bed, in case…well, just in case Nick's plans were upmarket.

'Mum,' Alison tried, 'about last night…'

'Let's forget about that,' Rose said. 'It's sorted now.'

Except it wasn't, Alison knew that. She looked

at her mum's strained face, at the panic that was always in her eyes, and it was more than Alison could deal with, more than she could help with, and she broached what she had once or twice before.

'Have you thought about talking to someone?' Alison swallowed. 'That grief counsellor you saw…'

'Can they bring them back?' Rose shook her head. 'Anyway, I'm fine. I am sorry about last night, I had no right to go through your things.'

'Mum,' Alison attempted, but the conversation was closed.

'What are you up to today?'

'I've no idea,' Alison admitted. 'Nick's planning something.'

And to Rose's credit she gave a bright smile. 'That sounds exciting.' But her smile faded as there was a low rumble in the street and as Rose went to the window she glanced anxiously at her daughter.

'Nick's here,' Rose said. 'On a bike.'

And, worse, he had two helmets.

'Hi, Rose.' Nick grinned. 'I'm taking Alison to Palm Beach—where they film that soap…'

'Nick…' She could see her mother's bleached face and knew she had to do something. 'I haven't been on a bike.'

'I'm the one riding it,' Nick said. 'All you have to do is hold on. Come on, Alison, I've got everything planned.'

The sun was in his eyes, so maybe he couldn't see her expression. Part of her knew she was being ridiculous, he was hardly going to go roaring off. It *should* have been the perfect surprise; it almost was. She wanted to grab the helmet he was offering, to climb on, to be the young woman she once had been, to spend a precious day with the man she adored.

So she tried.

'See you, Mum.'

'Alison, be ca—' And Rose tried too because she smothered down her warning. 'Have a good day.'

'I'll call you,' Alison promised, before her mum asked, and there was fear and trepidation but a certain exhilaration too as she took the helmet and did as he asked and just held on.

She held onto his back and felt the machine thrum into life, her lips tightly closed, breathing through her nose, utterly rigid as they made their way through the city and over the vast bridge. She wanted so many times to tell him to stop, to let her off, and yet there was a thrill, a thrill that felt almost like pure joy as they left the city behind. The bay glistened ever more beautiful with every turn, every incline, and Alison found out what it meant to leave her worries behind.

'Amazing, isn't it?' He paused the bike and they sat for a moment just admiring, and Alison waited for him to take a photo, but he didn't, he just sat and gazed out and drank it all in.

'We used to come here for a drive on Sundays,' Alison said. 'When we were kids,' she explained. 'If we go back a couple of kilo-metres, there's a nice picnic spot.'

'I've got it all worked out,' Nick said, turning the engine back on, and instead of going back they went on, further than she had been, and it felt faster too, but a faster that didn't unsettle her. She had her cheek pressed into his back, could feel the heat from his body and the blue of the water before her eyes and the wind on her legs and her hair whipping her mouth, and she wanted the road to last for ever.

Nick really had worked it out. He took the bike off the beaten path and he really had found the perfect spot. It was cool and mossy and a thick curtain of trees allowed no glimpse of the ocean, but you could hear the rumble of it in the background as they spread out the blanket and opened up the food.

'I couldn't sleep last night,' Nick admitted, opening up some wine as she scooped out rice onto plastic plates and shared out prawns. 'How about you?'

'It wasn't a great night…' Alison admitted, but she was reluctant to tell him about her mum, to bog him down with the endless problems, but *then* he surprised her.

'I couldn't sleep without you.'

And she tried not to let her heart leap, because then it would have to fall.

'I don't want this to end, Alison.' His eyes never moved, but his fingers found the knot of her bikini, his long slim fingers at the back of her neck, and she wanted to arch into them, but she just knelt there, felt the slight drop of her breasts as he unravelled the knot.

'Bet you say that to all your gals…' She tried to make a joke of it, but it petered out at the end. 'Here.' She pushed towards him a plate.

'I'm not hungry.'

Neither, suddenly, was she.

'Did you like the bike ride?'

'No,' Alison said.

'Liar.' Nick smiled, and it had all gone as planned, because that was supposed to be his lead in, something about bikes, he reminded himself, except his fingers had freed another knot now, and his train of thought was diverted as he peeled down her halter like the skin of a grape and saw the lovely plump flesh within, and maybe he was a little hungry after all.

'I couldn't sleep last night,' he repeated, but this time with different intent. And to others it might be tame, but to Alison it felt wild—she could feel the cool breeze on her breasts and she liked it, liked it more with each hot kiss he trailed because the breeze cooled her again. There was the hum of flies around neglected food and he kissed her off the blanket and away from them. She liked too the pillow of moss on her bottom as he slid her skirt up and in this, with him, there was no inhibition, and sometimes she wanted to explain, to tell him that this wasn't her, except in his arms it felt as if it was.

She slid down his zipper, slipped her hands inside and freed him, and such was her want she gave a sob of frustration as his hand slid to his trouser pocket, gritting her teeth and willing him to hurry it on, but it tore, and he cursed in frustration and dug in his pocket again. And she hated them so, with him, she hated them so, especially when they were in his wallet on the blanket, and there was a moment, not even a moment, where she looked in his eyes and there was a *Will we?* Only they never found out—a screech of brakes filled the warm air and a thud that had them both leaping up.

They were pulling at their clothes and Nick leapt on the bike and Alison did the same. 'It was that way,' Alison said, pointing left, and they headed along the cliff. She felt the slight wobble of the bike as his attention was diverted and her heart was already pumping faster before she saw it for herself—the front of a car crumpled into a tree and a man talking into his phone and waving frantically. Nick slowed down, pulling to a halt, and they both jumped off.

'I missed the bend,' the guy was shouting as they took off their helmets. 'I was going too fast, trying to get to the hospital, she suddenly wanted to push…'

It was so far better than it could have been, except Alison's heart wouldn't slow down.

'What's your name?' Nick asked as they ran to the car.

'Richard.' His wife's name was Carly and there was already an ambulance on the way, Richard told them.

Nick was assessing the passenger for injuries and apart from being in advanced labour, there appeared to be none.

'I'm only thirty-five weeks.'

'That's okay…' He was incredibly calm, unlike Alison. 'Thirty-five weeks is just fine. Alison, there's a first-aid box on the bike.' There was, the hire company had made sure of that, but her hands were shaking so much she could hardly open the clip, and in the end it was Nick who came over and waded through it. There wasn't much, but there were gloves and Nick pulled them on and told her to do the same then he headed back to the car and gave instructions.

'Alison.' She was aware he'd repeated it. 'Can you help me get Carly into the back?'

She helped the pregnant woman, rolled up a beach towel she found into a pillow and made her a bit more comfortable so she was semi-prone and though Richard was clearly beyond relieved there was a doctor present there was actually very little they needed to do, because nature was taking good care of both patients. All that was required from Nick were a few words of encouragement as he held the baby's head and guided the new life into the world.

'The head's out.' His voice was calm and Alison looked over his shoulder. She was holding Richard's T-shirt ready to wrap the babe, and it was all under control, except her heart was still thudding, she could feel the sun beating on her head and hear the distant blare of sirens. But the baby wasn't waiting for them—with just one final push the body was delivered and there was a bellow of rage from a rather small baby as Nick delivered it onto Carly's stomach.

'She's okay?' Carly checked, and Nick grinned.

'He's great.'

'I'm having a girl,' Carly insisted, pulling up her baby boy, but it was a happy mistake and from Richard's shout of joy, he wasn't complaining.

The arrival of the ambulance brought comfort rather than relief. Todd and his partner were wonderful with the new parents and baby. Richard cut the cord and then the paramedics transferred Carly to a stretcher.

Nick was on a high. There was a euphoria to him, and he stood with his arm around Alison as the stretcher was loaded into the ambulance.

'How good was that?' Nick grinned, with all

the joy of someone who finally, absolutely, definitely loved their job. 'How good was that?'

Only Alison didn't answer, uncomfortable suddenly as Todd climbed out from the back and closed the ambulance door and she wriggled out of Nick's arm, remembering they were keeping things away from work.

She could feel Todd's eyes roam her body, feel her breasts loose without a bra, and as, embarrassed, she ran a hand through her hair she felt leaves and knew, *knew* how she looked, knew what Todd was thinking.

'Nice work!' Todd winked at Nick when he'd closed the ambulance and Alison stood with her cheeks flaming. 'Good to get an easy one.'

'Thanks very much.' Nick shook his hand and all she could see as the ambulance drove away was the car against a tree and all she felt was reckless, and Alison loathed it. All she felt was a tart Nick had taken to the hills—so very easily, as Todd had pointed out.

'Thanks very much!' she hurled at him. 'Did you not hear what he was insinuating?'

'What?' Nick frowned.

'"Good to get an easy one"!'

'Alison.' Nick shook his head. 'He was talking about the birth.'

'No!' She felt sick, she actually felt sick. 'He was talking about me.'

And coming down from the high of the birth Nick started to see it, but Alison didn't want to hear his apology.

'I want to go home.'

'You're going to let what he said ruin—'

'It's already ruined,' Alison said. 'And even if we do patch it up, it will be ruined next week…'

'That's what I brought you here to talk about.' He hadn't meant to say it like this, hadn't meant to just blurt it out, but she left him with no choice. 'I'm going to ring work and tell them I'm not coming back early.' For Alison hope flared, but it was fleeting, so fleeting it was gone before it was recognised. 'I want to do Asia.'

She could have slapped him.

'With you,' Nick said quickly. 'I do have to go to this wedding in New Zealand but, look, I've been thinking about it…' All night he'd been thinking about it. He saw the flash of tears in her eyes, but he hadn't finished yet. 'Why don't you come—just for a few weeks, however much annual leave you've got…' He was finding this awkward, he knew she was proud. 'I know you must be stretched with the mortgage and everything, I'll sort out the tickets and things…' Alison screwed her eyes closed. 'We can have a couple of weeks away, just us.' And it sounded perfect, almost.

But then she'd have to come back.

'It's not that easy.'

'None of this is easy,' Nick said. 'Alison, surely you can have a holiday, a few weeks of fun.' And that word jolted, because that was what this was to him, she reminded herself, fun and a holiday that he wanted to extend—take the good sex with him, and slowly dismantle her heart. She wanted to nod, to say yes, to carry on the crazy ride, but she was scared to.

'I can't.' She shook her head in fury. 'I can't just up and leave.'

'Won't,' Nick said, and the pounding pulse in her head stopped for a second and he said it again. 'You won't come.'

'You don't know what you're talking about.' How dared he? Except Nick did.

'You didn't even consider it before you said no.'

'You don't know how hard things are for me. I had a massive row with my mother last night…'

Stunned, she watched as he pulled out an imaginary violin. 'You bastard.'

'You've had me pegged as one from the start.' Yes, he was being mean, but finally he was angry. 'I'm asking you to come with me, or at least to just think about coming with me.'

'And I'm telling you I can't.'

'You can't, can you?' Finally he got it. 'It's not your mum holding you back, Alison.'

'Just leave it.'

'No.' He couldn't and he wouldn't. 'It's not just your mum.'

'Let's just finish it.' If she was being unreasonable, well, she felt unreasonable. 'Let's just finish it here.'

And she did.

When the police arrived and summoned a tow truck, and a couple pulled over in their car and asked if there was anything they could do—actually, there was something.

'Could you give me a lift, please?'

CHAPTER FOURTEEN

IT HAD to be better this way, Alison told herself as she ignored Nick's texts over the next few days and tried to get used to lugging around a broken heart.

The dazzling blond doctor was a just a little less so over the coming week.

Tired, a bit distracted and to the rest of the team just a little less fun, but he was thorough and kind to the patients and sometimes, quite a lot actually, she felt his eyes follow hers, and sometimes they frowned just a touch when their eyes met, because the Alison he had known simply wasn't there any more.

He was kicking himself, angry with himself about how he had handled it. But he was angry with her too—at how readily she could let them go, at how she just retreated back into her quiet, serious shell. Though she was polite and smiled and spoke when she had to, the Alison he knew was in there seemed to have gone.

'I'm getting nowhere.' Amy was unusually tense as she handed over her night to Nick. 'This poor man came in at three—he's an oncology patient with a brain tumour, but he's got acute abdomen. He had a scan last week in Outpatients that was apparently all clear, the surgeons don't want him to have anything till they've seen him, but they're doing an aneurism repair we had in—'

'So he's had nothing for pain?' Nick checked sharply.

'Five of morphine,' Amy said. 'I couldn't ask him to wait any longer, but it hasn't touched sides, and the second-on surgeons are in Theatre as well.' It was a regular scenario—the surgeons couldn't asses an acute abdomen if the patient was pain free, but the surgeons were stuck in Theatre. 'I can't get his notes, he was seen in Outpatients last week…'

Amy really was frazzled—and from the nursing handover it made sense. It had been an extremely busy night, but nothing usually fazed Amy. Still, Alison remembered she had swapped her nights with Nick for a family thing a few weeks ago and guessed that maybe it had something to do with things.

'If they're in Theatre it's not going to be this team that takes him.' Nick was completely reasonable. He looked up at the medical roster. 'I'll ring Howard's team—he's on take today and I'll get one of them to come down before they start rounds. I'll go and have a quick look at him now.

'Alison,' he added, because she was cleaning up the night staff's chaos, because she was the only one around, because he had to, 'can you come with me?'

'His daughter, Vivienne, is getting upset,' Amy added.

'I'll sort it,' Nick replied. 'Go home,' he ordered.

'Thanks,' Amy said. 'What will we do without you?'

Nick could have sworn he felt the roll of Alison's eyes, but chose to ignore it, heading for the cubicle instead. 'Hi, I'm Nick. I'm an emergency registrar…'

'So was the other one!' A woman, presumably Vivienne, snapped. 'Where are the surgeons?'

'I'm going to speak with today's team,' Nick said, 'but first I need to take a quick look for myself at your father.'

Jim was frail, thin and clearly in pain, and Nick didn't prod and poke him unnecessarily, but he agreed with Amy's finding that the problem was acute—because even if Jim's condition was terminal, an operation might be needed to relieve his pain.

'I need those old notes,' Nick said once they were outside the cubicle.

'The day receptionist is here,' Alison said, 'and Outpatients will be opening. I'll ask her to track them down.'

'Thanks.' He hesitated. 'Alison?'

'Yes?'

'Are you okay?'

'I'm fine,' Alison said.

'Can we talk?'

'About work?' she checked, and when he pushed his tongue into his cheek, she shrugged. 'Then sorry, no,' Alison said, and headed for Reception.

'How's the flat?' Another line she was getting used to. Libby, the receptionist, asked the question as Alison popped in to check on the location of Jim's notes.

'Shabbier than I remember it,' Alison admitted. 'I'm painting before I move in and I don't remember a pea-green carpet when I bought it, but it must have been there.'

'Are you replacing it?' They stood making idle chit-chat as Libby tapped away on the computer and did her best to locate the notes Nick wanted.

'I was going to learn to live with it,' Alison said, 'but the more I paint, the greener it gets.'

'You'll get there,' Libby said, and then she shook her head. 'Those notes can't have come back from Outpatients.'

'They really need them,' Alison said. 'He's been seen by Gastro and the surgeons and they're all passing him on. He needs to be sorted. The family's getting really frustrated and frankly I don't blame them. Can you ring them again?'

'For all the good it will do.' Libby rolled her eyes. 'I'll go over now and have a look myself,' she offered. 'Could you just take these through for me?' She handed Alison a couple of rosters but as Alison walked through, the family caught her.

'Did you get his notes?'

'The receptionist is going to go over to Outpatients now—' She didn't get to finish. Jim's daughter let out several hours of frustration in a few caustic sentences, and Alison stood there, shaking her head a touch as a security man started to walk over.

'I know how hard this must be—'

'You know nothing,' Vivienne retorted. 'That's my father suffering in there, not that you care. Did you enjoy your coffee break? He hasn't had a drink since he arrived, he's sobbing for some water—'

'Vivienne.' Nick came over, gave Alison a tight, grim smile. 'Let's take this to an interview room.' He'd cut right in and Alison was grateful for it, annoyed with herself for not suggesting the same thing but glad that someone else was dealing with it. Alison glanced down at them as she popped the medical rosters on the bench. They were nothing to do with her, just the doctors rosters for the next four weeks, and normally she wouldn't have given them thought. Except today, she scanned the sheet and saw the absence of Nick's name, saw that Cort Mason was, in fact, coming back, and it just rammed home the truth. There it was, in black and white, as if she needed reminding, that in just a few days Nick Roberts would be gone.

'She apologises.' Nick came over to make a phone call. 'She's going to say it herself—'

'There's no need.'

She was close to tears all of a sudden but was determined not to let him see. 'Libby's gone over to Outpatients to try and find them—he was there last week.'

'He should have been admitted last week,' Nick said, and then, a little more tactfully, he told the voice on the end of the phone the same thing, and as Alison went to go he caught her wrist, which was the most physical he had ever been at work and the only contact in days. And she couldn't bear it, yet she took it, waited as he concluded his call, Nick doodling on the hateful rosters as he spoke on the phone.

'They're going to admit him.' He gave her the details and then there was just a slight frown as he looked her over and she didn't like his scrutiny.

'Are you really okay?'

'I'll get over you, Nick, don't worry.' She

didn't turn round, because for the first time since his arrival, the first time in years in fact, there were tears, not just in her eyes but trickling down her cheeks, and Alison fled to the toilets, blew her nose and told herself she was being stupid, told herself she'd warned herself that this would happen.

'Alison?' Ellie was just dashing in before the start of her late shift, the surprise evident in her voice at catching her friend less than strong, because over the years she'd never seen her cry. 'Are you okay?'

'I'm tired,' she admitted, because suddenly she was. 'And there's this poor man, he's been shoved from pillar to post. He's been here since two this morning and we've only just found him a bed, his daughter just went off at me—'

'I know,' Ellie said, because anyone who worked in Emergency did know that families sometimes took out their frustration on the closest target, and even if Vivienne hadn't been that bad, some days it just hurt.

'All okay?' Sheila, the NUM, came in then and Alison even managed a wry smile that her *escape* to the loos had become so public and made a little note to herself not to go into meltdown till she was safely in a cubicle.

'A relative upset her,' Ellie explained.

'It's not just that,' Alison admitted. 'I don't feel so great.'

'You don't look so great,' Sheila said, and because it was Alison, who was always stoic, she knew it wasn't an excuse. 'Why don't you take a half-day? What are you on tomorrow?'

'An early.'

'Go home.' Sheila was firm and fair and knew how hard her staff worked. 'If you don't feel any better this evening, give us a call so we can arrange cover tomorrow.'

Alison felt more than a little guilty as she collected her bag, because even if she was tired and teary, there was another reason for it. The bus took for ever, it just crawled along and stopped at every stop. Maybe she was more than tired, she decided, trudging up the street to her house. Maybe she was getting the flu or something.

It was Tuesday, because the house smelt like beef stroganoff as she entered, though it smelt stronger today. Alison headed for her room, but the smell was in there too, permeating the whole house. She opened a window, swallowing a couple of times, and then fled to the loo, which was thankfully a lot quieter than the one at work.

'No.'

She actually said it out loud as she headed back to the bedroom, climbed into bed and very deliberately blocked that thought, and blocked it again when her mum came home and Alison had to fly back to the bathroom again.

'I think I've got gastro,' Alison said, and there were benefits to living at home, because she got some water, then tea and toast all brought to her, and her mum rang up Sheila to say that she wasn't well and wouldn't be in tomorrow.

You okay? I heard you were sick.

She read his text at ten p.m. and didn't reply.

Just turned on her side and tried to get to sleep.

She truly didn't know what to say.

CHAPTER FIFTEEN

'YOU look terrible.' Ellie breezed into her bedroom on her way to a late shift. 'Or are you just not wearing mascara?'

'Both.' Alison tried to smile.

'Alison…' Ellie was tentative for once. 'I can see that you and Nick…well, you both look pretty miserable.' As quiet as they'd kept it, of course Ellie knew. 'I'm assuming it's over?'

'It was always going to be.'

'I'm sorry,' Ellie said. 'I feel like I pushed you into it…'

'I pushed myself into it,' Alison admitted.

'You can talk to me.'

'I know,' Alison said. 'Just not yet.'

'It's his leaving do on Friday. I just thought I should warn you…'

'I'm on days off Thursday and Friday,' Alison said, 'and I'm off sick today. I won't be seeing him again.'

And that was hard to say, let alone admit, and she couldn't really talk about it with Ellie—they were just different personalities, Ellie so light and breezy, she herself so serious. She'd been a fool to think she could do a relationship any other way. Surprisingly it was Rose who bought comfort, bringing her in some lunch and sitting on the bed for a while.

'I went and saw Anna,' Rose said, 'that grief counsellor…' The bite of scrambled egg stilled in her mouth as Rose spoke on. 'I was shocked by what happened, that I could hit you…' She started to cry a bit and Alison held her hand. 'I already had Tim by the time I was your age—and despite what I told your father, what I've told myself enough over the years, he wasn't actually my first.'

Alison was shocked, especially when Rose continued.

'Or my second.'

'Enough information!' Alison smiled.

'I've been holding you back for my own selfish reasons and you've been a wonderful daughter, Alison…but you need your life too.' And she told her what Nick had. 'You're holding back too.'

'No.' Alison shook her head and Rose, as she often did, rammed home her point. 'What's happening with Nick?'

'He leaves on Sunday,' Alison said. 'We had a bit of a row.' She took a deep breath. 'He offered to fly me out to Asia—do some travelling with him, just for a few weeks. It's not that simple, though.'

'Can you afford it?' Rose asked, and Alison was so proud of how she was trying—so relieved to have such a long-awaited *real* conversation with her mum.

'He offered to pay,' Alison said. 'It should be cheap—he's going right off the beaten track…'

'You'd need some immunisations…'

Alison shook her head. 'It's not the money, Mum. I don't want to feel like this again in a few weeks. I just want it over with, I just want him gone.' And she couldn't even cry because she wanted to be sick, which she was, dashing across the hall and just making it to the loo as Rose stood outside, fretting.

'Maybe just stick with toast.'

And Alison didn't answer, just leant over the loo and closed her eyes, because it wasn't scrambled egg making her sick, and it wasn't her mother or money stopping her from following her heart now, it wasn't even her.

She was in no position to be getting immunisations and going off the beaten track.

No position at all.

Of that, she was almost certain.

CHAPTER SIXTEEN

SHE'D bought several pregnancy tests from this chemist without giving it a thought. Ellie panicked on regular occasions, but now that the test was for herself, she felt as if she knew half the shop and was sure the girl serving was the daughter of one of her mum's friends, though hopefully she didn't recognise her.

They'd been careful, Alison told herself as she took her little parcel home.

But not quite careful enough, Alison realised as she stared at the little blue cross. And maybe it was coincidence, but as her mind drifted to Nick, his must have drifted to her, because she felt the buzz of her phone.

Can I see you before I go?

Still sick, Alison replied.

I can come over. Do you need anything?

She was tempted to text back *Pram, cot, nappies,* but instead she wrapped all the evidence back up in a paper bag, put that inside a carrier bag and then in another one and then put it in the outside bin before she texted him back the absolute truth.

I need space.

CHAPTER SEVENTEEN

'YOU missed a great night!' Moira was at her most bubbly, so too was everyone else as Alison dragged herself into work. 'Nick knows how to have a good time.'

It was all she heard all morning.

How great the party had been, how much everyone would miss him, and Alison couldn't face the staffroom on her lunch break, so instead she slipped outside to the little patch of grass behind Emergency, sat in the sun and tried not to think that this time tomorrow he would be on a plane.

There was no question that she must tell him.

The baby was his, he had a right to know,

and their child had a right to know about its father too.

And, yes, Alison thought as she closed her eyes and the sun warmed her skin, it would be more sensible by far to have this difficult conversation face to face, but it would be so much easier another way.

She could plan what she said better, Alison told herself, tried to convince herself.

He needed to know that there would be no pressure on him.

It was her choice to keep the baby.

It would be better by email, Alison decided, then wavered. The truth was she couldn't stand to see his reaction as she crushed all his dreams.

'Am I disturbing you?' Amy sat on the bench beside her.

'Not at all,' Alison said.

'I just wanted a bit of peace.' Amy gave a tired smile. 'I've got so much going on at the moment and they're all…' Her voice trailed off for a moment. 'I'm going to miss Nick,' she said, and Alison looked, really looked, and saw a flash of tears in the registrar's eyes. Then Amy's phone bleeped and she looked down and smiled as she read the text.

'Speak of the devil.'

This time Alison made sure she was actually *in* the toilet cubicle when she had her little meltdown.

She was overreacting, she told herself, and yet…and yet… Amy had been acting differently lately and she and Nick did get on.

What? her angry brain demanded. When she had gone home to her mum's, had Amy come round?

Had Nick told Amy to keep things quiet too?

Oh, God!

Up came her coffee and half a slice of toast and down came the tears.

She needed her head straight, needed to *really* think this through before she told him.

Somehow she got through the rest of the day. Amy shut herself in her office, no doubt to cry over him, Alison thought savagely.

By the time she was on the bus-ride home she had visions of Amy and herself stuck together in the same maternity ward.

Hell, maybe Moira would be there too.

'Alison!' She nearly jumped out of skin as she stepped off the bus and Nick was waiting for her. 'I was hoping we could talk. I don't want to leave with things as they are,' Nick said, as she walked along silently beside him. 'I don't want it to end on this note…'

It wasn't going to!

They walked down the road and he suggested something to eat, which was the last thing she wanted. 'Can we just sit?'

So they sat on a bench and watched the world go by for a moment.

'Alison, I don't know what happened,' Nick admitted. 'I know you think the paramedic insinuated something—I didn't see it as that. Alison, if I had thought for a moment… Do you really think I'd let someone speak about you like that?'

'How will you speak of me?' Her eyes glittered with challenge. 'When you're showing your photos, how are you going to describe me?'

'Confusing,' Nick said, 'because sometimes I feel closer to you than I ever have to anyone and other times…'

Nick was very easy to talk to, it was she that wasn't. She was concentrating so hard on not crying, on not challenging him, on just getting through, she hardly said a word.

'Will you please at least think about Asia?' Nick said to her silence.

'I can't go to Asia.'

'Alison, if it's the money…'

'It's not the money,' Alison gulped, 'it's…' And she bit down on her lips, because she needed to know how she felt before she shared it with him, needed just a moment's pause before everything in her life suddenly changed.

'Just go, Nick.'

'Just like that?' he challenged.

'Just like that,' she confirmed.

And because it had just been a few weeks, because there was no baggage, because he was just moving on, he took her at her word and stood, and so did Alison.

'Do you want to keep in touch?' Nick offered, because the poor man had no idea what was coming, no idea just how in touch they'd need to be.

And she didn't say a word, just nodded, and because she had to, it was Alison who walked away.

'You okay, darling?'

'Yes. Sorry I was late, I went to the flat.'

'You're not at work, Alison,' the new Rose said. 'You don't have to apologise for being late. How's the flat looking?'

'Orchid white.' Alison gave a wry smile. 'I've finished the lounge, I'm going back tomorrow to do a couple of other rooms, but it looks like an indoor tennis centre with that carpet.'

'It will be fine once it's got the furniture in,' Rose said, and then sat down. 'You know, I've been looking at some brochures…' She handed one to Alison and for just a second Alison wondered if she knew, because there were pictures of London and her mind jumped for a moment, then swung back as Rose faltered on. 'Your father and I always spoke about doing a trip to Europe, taking a couple of months…' And then Alison looked at the brochure, really looked, and, as she seemed to be doing rather a lot lately, tried to keep the tears from coming. 'It's for over-fifties, for widows, divorcees… It's not a meeting thing,' Rose said primly. 'They just sort out the accommodation, it's company…'

'It sounds wonderful,' Alison said.

'I want my life back too.' Rose was the one crying now. 'I want to do the things that I always said I would.'

'And you should.'

'There's a cancellation,' Rose said, and Alison realised then that her mother wasn't just thinking about it, she really was going to do it. 'But I'd have to go in three weeks. I've got enough annual leave stored up.'

'Go for it,' Alison said, and kissed her mum. 'You might need help with the flat and—'

'Mum!' Alison kept her voice light but firm. 'You have to go.'

And they spent an hour looking on the computer at all the places Rose would visit, all the things she would finally do, and Alison was pleased, more than pleased for her mother, but there was a hollow sadness there too. The conversation, the row that she had staved off for so long—now, she wished she could have had it sooner, because now everyone was moving on and *she* was the one who was…

Stuck.

She tried to reframe it, tried to rephrase it.

Pregnant, with a mortgage.

She tried and she tried and she tried once again, but no matter how she tried, as she walked into her new home the next day, there was only one other word she could think of—*trapped.*

Was it wrong to feel trapped?

Was *trapped* even the right word?

There was another word there, an emotion there that she didn't want to examine, so instead Alison slapped orchid-white paint on the walls and felt like the worst person in the world, because this wasn't how it was supposed to be, this wasn't how she was supposed to feel.

Except she did.

She stared at what was going to be her study, and even that had been a concession, a trauma course instead of a journey, but now even that was looking impossible.

A nursery.

She'd laughed when the real estate agent had said it, he had been so completely off track, yet just a few weeks later that was exactly what it was about to become.

And she stood in the little room and tried hard to picture it.

Staggering in for two a.m. feeds.

She actually could, she could see herself all dishevelled and exhausted and stressed, just like Shelly, could see a pink, screaming baby and a lonely flat and a fridge stuck with postcards from Daddy.

Or worse, far worse for Alison, would be the sight of Nick in the doorway, unshaved and annoyed, and trying to snatch some sleep because he was on call, and just so removed from his own dream…

She slapped the paint onto the wall.

She'd rather, far rather, far, far rather, do it alone.

Which she did.

She got the main bedroom done, and the kitchen and all the lights were blazing until late in the night. And despite what she'd said, a part of her hoped for a knock at the door, for the space she'd insisted on to be suddenly filled, but Nick had clearly taken her at her word.

The smell of paint made her sick, so late in the evening she walked the short walk home, along the foreshore, and she couldn't help what she did next. Maybe she was a stalker, but she took a little diversion past where Nick was staying and the lights were off and, yes, he could be out, but there was something about an empty home, and Alison knew then he had gone. She took a deep breath and thought about the little bean-sized thing in her womb, the baby he had unwittingly left behind.

'Can you do me a favour?' Her voice was a bit shaky and she should perhaps have apologised to Ellie for ringing her so late, but she was frantic.

'Sure.'

'Can you tell me your Facebook password?'

'It says never to reveal your password to anyone.' Ellie laughed and then promptly revealed it. 'Don't you want him to know you're watching?'

'You know me too well.'

There was a pause, a tiny pause. 'You know that he's…' Her voice trailed off and Ellie sat in silence on the phone as Alison, with a few short clicks, found out Nick was in New Zealand.

'Are you okay, Alison?'

'I'm fine,' Alison said, then relented, admitting a little of her truth. 'It just hurts more than it should. I mean, I knew it wasn't for ever, I knew it could only be short term…' She couldn't believe he'd gone. Okay, she'd asked him to, but he really was, grinning from the top of a rock in his profile picture, like that cat that had got the cream, and here she was, feeling as if she was on the top of a rock, but without the safety harness.

She waited till her mum went to bed then sat with a big mug of tea, and it felt different clicking on his profile without Ellie over her shoulder, peering into his life and scrolling through to find out more about the man she loved.

He was more social than her by far.

There were school friends, friends from med school and not just cyber friends. They were in his life, joking with him to get a job, asking when he'd be back, missing him at football and concerts and nights out, and that was aside from family.

And there was Moira.

Missing him already *and* she'd added a kiss.

And she hoped to catch up with him in Asia.

And there was Gillian, who still messaged him—pretty, funny and patient.

His status was single.

And that hurt.

So too was the fact he never mentioned her—that their ride to Palm Beach, their one massive row was just described as 'an interesting day'.

There was a life and a family and friends and a whole world waiting for him on the other side of the world, and on this side there was Alison and the little bean-sized thing growing inside that she was trying to get used to.

And maybe she really was a stalker, because she scrolled through Ellie's friends and then Nick's and there was no sign of Amy.

And then he updated.

Back from sampling local delights. Great to meet cousins—loving it here.

This probably wasn't the best place to announce a pregnancy, so she contained herself and clicked off and then she went up to bed and lay with her flat stomach and tried to be nice to it.

'We'll be okay,' Alison said, in a voice that didn't sound entirely convinced.

CHAPTER EIGHTEEN

ALISON *was* sensible.

The world should have been back where it had been two months ago, except a blond English doctor had upended her life and now she somehow had to put it back.

She chose not to tell her mum, because she didn't want Rose not to take her trip.

But she took folate and saw her GP and then later an obstetrician, who scanned her and told her she was ten weeks pregnant, and she was about to correct him, because Nick had only been gone for two weeks, then remembered that it was dated from the start of her cycle.

And she had to tell him; she'd tried to tell him.

There were about fifty attempts in the draft

box of her email and she'd rung three times but hung up before it could connect.

Tonight.

Alison decided as she put on her lanyard and checked all her pens. Tonight she would ring him, before he headed for Asia.

Or maybe, a little voice said as she smiled at Ellie, who was on her way home from night shift, she should wait till he's there.

'God, I hate nights,' Ellie said, and then she looked at her friend. 'You look awful.'

'I shifted my stuff yesterday and I'm trying to help Mum pack for her trip—sleep is a distant memory.'

'Here.' Ellie handed over her make-up bag. 'You'll scare the patients.'

She so could not be bothered with make-up, but Ellie was right—she did look terrible—so Alison retied her hair and put on some mascara and a bit of lip gloss, and when Ellie doused herself in perfume she squirted some at her friend.

'Still missing him?' Ellie asked, but Alison just gave a noncommittal shrug.

'The best way to get over a man is to get under another.' Ellie grinned. 'And you've no hope looking like that.'

'Thanks for the sage advice.'

'You *will* thank me.' Ellie beamed. 'Come on, you're late and I'm skiving off early.'

They walked out together, talking much about nothing, and then the world stopped because there at the nurses' station was Nick, smiling as she walked over. Her heart was in her mouth and her face must have paled but thank God for Ellie, who had ensured she was at least wearing mascara!

'Hi, there,' he said as she stood waiting for handover.

'Hi.' Alison could hardly get the word out,

her throat was squeezed closed so tightly. 'How was New Zealand?'

'Great.'

And he just stood and she just looked and he just waited—and there were so many things that she wanted to say, to ask, and so much she wanted to avoid, so awkwardly she just stood.

'Nick!' Sheila was far more effusive. 'What on earth? It is so good to see you—we've had to battle through with the most miserable locum in the southern hemisphere.' She glanced over her shoulder just in case he was around, then shrugged. 'How long till you disappear?'

'Not sure,' Nick said. 'I've got a few things I need to sort out.'

He *did* change the energy of the place.

Moira squealed in delight when she came on at midday and though he was holed up an awful lot in Amy's office, Alison tried not to be jealous, or get ahead of herself and believe that it was *them* he had come to sort out. And yet, as she showed around a new group of student nurses, she was reminded of a certain matter that needed discussing.

'X-ray.' The familiar call came from Resus, and Alison moved the group back.

'Just be careful,' Alison warned. 'They do call out, but just be aware that there are a lot of portable X-rays taken here.'

'Is Resus lead lined?' a student asked, and Alison shook her head.

'You just need to keep your distance when they're shooting, and wear a gown.' She knew it was safe, had pored over all the information, knew that the safest place to stand was behind the radiographer, and that, really, the level of exposure was tiny, and yet, and yet… 'If you're pregnant, or think there's a chance you might be, it's best to let us know if you're not happy to be in there when they're taking films.' And then Alison realised just how futile those words were and offered the next best thing. 'Or just slip away…'

Which she tried to do when her shift ended, but Nick caught her as she slunk off.

'I want a word with you.' He was waiting outside the changing room. 'Several, in fact. If you want to, that is.' And she didn't know what she wanted so he spoke into the silence. 'I know a nice café that does ricotta cheese and cherry strudel—I'll be there at five.'

He was there before her again.

Only her teeth didn't feel like glass. Instead her mouth felt like it was filled with sand as she made her way over.

'I've already ordered,' Nick said as a waitress came over.

'I might not have come.'

'I'm always hungry.' They sat in silence as

two lattés and two strudels were placed before them and Alison took a sip of her drink.

'What happened, Alison?'

And she had to tell him, except the words wouldn't come out.

So she toyed with her strudel, and went to take a bite, then remembered that soft cheese was on the list of forbidden foods her obstetrician had given her, and as she put the pastry down she saw him frown, almost saw the thought process in his eyes. And then two words were said, presumably by her, because it sounded like her voice and Nick's lips weren't moving.

And then she closed her eyes, because she didn't want to see all his dreams evaporating, didn't want to witness him realise that his twelve months of freedom had just delivered him every last thing he'd been trying to avoid.

'When did you find out?' His voice sounded normal.

'A few days ago.' Alison swallowed. 'When I was sick.'

'That was more than a few days ago, that was a few *weeks* ago, Alison.'

'I'm sorry.' Only Nick wasn't cross with her for not telling him.

'You shouldn't have been holding this in on your own.' He dragged a hand through his hair. 'I knew there was something wrong. I thought it was the promotion, me leaving…'

It was.

And it was a whole lot more too.

'You *could* have told me,' Nick said.

Not *should*, for which she was grateful. 'I was trying to sort out what I want.'

'And what do you want?'

'I don't know,' Alison admitted. 'I won't have an abortion so I guess it's not really about that…' She wasn't making much sense, but she didn't care. 'If you're feeling trapped, believe me, you're not alone.'

'I never said I was feeling trapped.'

'Oh, please.' She was angry, not at him but at the world. 'Well, I do. I haven't even left home and guess what—now I probably won't be able to. I'll end up renting the flat out. Mum can babysit while I work.' She could feel the walls closing in, she absolutely could see the walls closing in as she envisaged the future.

'You don't think I'd support you.'

That just made her crosser.

'Oh, yes, that's right, you're so Mr PC that you'll send a lovely cheque for his schooling and we'll fly over to you once year or you'll come here and we'll be all civil—'

'Alison,' he interrupted, 'did it never enter your head that I'd stay, that we could do this together?' And that just made her crosser still because, yes, of course it had entered her head, and now he was suggesting it, it just made it harder because she didn't want it to be that way, didn't want to force his hand, didn't want the man who had come here for fun and to find himself, a man who so clearly didn't want to settle down, to be forced to.

'You'll resent me,' she said, shuddered it out, the most horrible of all her horrible thoughts. 'You might never say it, you might never show it, but I'll know. I'll always know that if it wasn't for the baby…'

'Alison—'

She didn't let him finish. 'Please, do us both a favour, go on your adventure, have your trip, have your fun, and if you have an epiphany somewhere in Nepal—'

'Nepal?' For the first time he bordered on sounding cross. 'Are we talking about your dream holiday or mine? Alison, I'm not going to just get on a plane—'

'Please do!' She struggled not to shout. 'And if fatherhood and babies and maternity bras and nappies suddenly appeal, I'll still be here, getting bigger and fatter, and we can sort something out. Or you can head back to London and we can sort something out from there, but right now I want space, I want time, I want to work out my future, so please go and live yours.'

'You really want space.'

'Yes.' Could she make it any clearer? 'I want to get my head around this myself, and I can't do that with you.'

CHAPTER NINETEEN

HE GAVE her space and she loathed him for it.

He spoke politely at work, and he didn't text, or ring, or email.

There was one room left to do in the flat and she couldn't face it.

Could not go in and again picture a cot, so she opened up her laptop on the disgusting green carpet and logged in as Ellie again and tortured herself with his latest postings.

He was back to earn more money, apparently.

And one of the many that jarred was a response to a question from Gillian.

Bangkok here I come!

'It's me and you,' she said to the slight curve on her stomach—and she slapped paint on her baby's wall and refused to wait for Nick's epiphany to come. She would keep on keeping on.

But when she had her first ever ring on her own doorbell, she didn't feel so sure.

He was blond and unshaven and looking just a bit fed up with his lot.

'Just how much space do you need, Alison?' he asked. 'Because this is driving me crazy. You can't just ignore it.'

'I'm not ignoring it.'

'No one knows—I saw you lifting a patient, all the X-rays in Resus…'

'I go out,' Alison said. 'I wear a lead gown.'

'Does your mum know?'

'Not yet. I'm not keeping it from her,' Alison said. 'Well, I am, but she's going on holiday, I don't want to ruin it.' And she burst into tears. 'Like I ruined yours.'

'You haven't ruined anything,' Nick said, and she couldn't even begin to believe him.

'I'm crazy about you. I have been since that bus ride.'

'Oh, please…' And out it came then, all the pent-up insecurity, all the doubts, all the things she'd stored up and tried to pretend didn't matter.

'You're single online,' she flung it at him. 'Off out, having *fun*—' she tossed that word up at him '—delivering babies up mountains, climbing bridges, and not a single mention of me…'

'Alison…' He was trying not to smile, and it incensed her. 'You're single, I can see that in the small part of the profile you allow to be visible, and you won't even be my friend…' He nudged her, tried to pull her from her tears as if they were in the school playground.

'No!' She was furious, close, dangerously close, to painting a gloss ochre strip on his suit with the paintbrush she pointed at him. 'I don't go on there.' Well, she did, all the time lately, but she wasn't actively on there was what she would say if challenged, but she was on a roll now. 'You say you're crazy about me, that you can't stop thinking about me, but you're on there every night, and I seem to slip your mind every time.' And then she burst into hears as she recited his latest posting. 'Bangkok here I come!'

He laughed.

He had the audacity to laugh, but not at her, Alison realised, because in the middle of hell she actually laughed too, a laugh that was laced with tears but a laugh anyway. 'You're such a bastard.'

'But I'm not.' He shook his head. He rued his words and the pain he had caused her, but he knew at least that he could put that bit right. 'I'm not a bastard, Alison, I'm not even a good backpacker, I'm the worst backpacker. That person you're reading about…' And she watched him struggle to explain it. 'Do you know how hard it was to justify taking a year off? Do you know how hard it was to end a very good relationship, for no good reason?'

And she did, she did.

'It seemed incredibly important to…' He raked his hand through his hair. 'To cram everything in, to have a ball, to validate…' Then he was completely serious. 'And I've loved doing all those things, but the bit I've loved most is the photos, is the afterwards, is sitting on the balcony with you. I can't tell her I'm no longer single on a computer, that's a face to face, or a difficult phone call at the very least, and I wouldn't do that to Gillian. I honestly didn't know you were looking, or I'd have explained…' She shook her head, sick of his smooth talk, not wanting to be a woman who just believed because it was safer. It annoyed him, she could tell, so much so that he opened his laptop and she ignored him, carried on painting the wall as he logged on.

Not sure about Bangkok. Alison is pregnant, but she hasn't told her mum yet and we're not sure what to do. That bloody ride to Palm Beach was awful. I had meant to tell her I was serious and we spend some time overseas to get to know each other more. She got all stroppy and hitchhiked a lift home, she was completely mental...

'Do you want me to post it?'

She just stood there and read over his shoulder.

'Do you see that the person you've read about isn't all of me?'

She could.

'That there are other sides?' She nodded. 'I rang Gillian.' Alison felt her world still. 'I told her about you, because even though we're over, even though it ended more than six months ago—' and she got what he was saying '—she didn't need to read about it first.'

'I know.'

'And there's something else you should know,' Nick said, 'which you might not like and you might not understand. But I told her about the baby too. I know there are other people we need to tell…'

And she didn't like it, because it confirmed her darkest fears.

'It gives you the reason to stay.'

'I've already got a reason,' Nick said. 'I already had a reason.' He pulled her close. 'You.' Then he ran a hand over her stomach. 'This one just speeds up the decision-making process.'

'It's not what you wanted.'

'Not with Gillian,' Nick said. 'Alison, I don't believe in accidents.'

'So I meant it to happen.'

'I don't mean that.'

'You work in Accident and Emergency, you're going to be consultant when you get back…' Her voice was rising. 'And you're standing here telling me that you don't believe in accidents.' She was incensed now. 'What? Do you think my father and brother secretly wanted to die, that they deliberately—?'

'I mean *this* sort of accident…' He closed his eyes. 'I'm not saying this very well.'

'No, Nick, you're not.' She couldn't believe what she was hearing. 'You really think I set out to—'

'No.' He interrupted. 'No.' He said it again.

'Then what?'

'We knew,' Nick said. 'We, more than anyone, knew. And, yes, we were careful, but not *that* careful.'

And she opened her mouth to argue, but nothing came out, because she'd been over and over and over their oh, so careful love-making, except sometimes it hadn't been. Sometimes passion had overruled common sense and she was very cross with herself for that. With Paul she'd been contracepted to the neck, if there was such a word. With Paul she could have raged at the sky, at the gods, at the injustice, because she had been so very, very careful, but with Nick… She screwed her eyes closed, because the only person she was raging at was herself.

'I knew the risks too.' He caught her racing brain and sent it on a different track. 'Oh, I wasn't actively thinking…' The words weren't coming easily for Nick, but he was at least trying, this conversation incredibly honest, dangerously honest perhaps. 'I'm responsible, Alison, I've *never* not been careful except with you.' And it was raw and honest and the truth. 'And, yes, I should have taken more care, you can throw that at me too if you want to, but I guess for the first time passion won. There was someone, you, that I was willing not to be so practical and sensible with…' And he looked at her then and stated a fact. 'That's how babies are made, have been since the beginning of time. The chance was worth it at the time.'

'Is it worth it now?'

'Of course it is.' He sounded very sure.

'You want to travel.'

'The world will still be there, waiting.' And then he grinned. 'To tell you the truth, I'm sick of throwing myself off cliffs. You've saved me another bungee-jump, yet another sodding extreme sport to show I'm having a good time.'

'What will your parents say?' Alison asked.

'Trapped by a colonial!' He rolled his eyes. 'They'll come round. I know you can't leave her, Alison, and I completely see why.'

'What about your job?'

'I've got a job! I've been offered a year's work when Amy goes on maternity leave next week.'

And he gave a little grimace. 'Keep that quiet—I mean it. She's adopting a baby from overseas and she's beside herself—doesn't want to tell anyone till he's actually here.'

And someone *was* looking after her, because Nick would never need to know how little she had trusted him, how this gorgeous blonde sexy doctor somehow really was just that.

'What about your mum?'

'She'll be completely and utterly delighted.' And there was a wobble in her voice, a strange fizz of excitement that had, till now, when she thought of the baby been absent, a vision, a glimpse of a future, only now she could see Nick and herself and a beach and a baby…

And then she admitted something, something she hadn't dared admit, not even to herself.

'I'm scared.'

'I know.'

'No, you don't,' Alison said. 'It's not trapped that I feel, it's…'

'Scared,' he offered, and she nodded, sure he didn't really get it, except it would seem he did. 'Scared you might love it too much?' he said, and she nodded. 'Scared you might lose it?'

And he shouldn't say that, Alison thought frantically, because if he said it, then maybe it would happen.

'I think being a parent means you're scared for the rest of your life.'

'I can't stand what my mum went through.'

'Then you've got a choice,' Nick said. 'You can hold back, never fully live, never fully love, just in case…' Which was what she had been doing. 'But that doesn't work, because sooner or later living wins. Look at your mum,' Nick went on. 'Look at you.' He put his hand on her stomach, the result of taking a chance, and he was right because, cautious or not, life threw in surprises whether you liked them or not.

'I got you a present.'

And out of his laptop bag he produced not a ring but a rather tatty airplane magazine folded on one page. And it was nicer than a ring, nicer than anything actually, because it was a flight map showing all the destinations that airline went to, and Nick pointed a couple of them out.

'There's Sydney,' he said, 'and there's London, and there's an awful lot of world in between. You choose the stopovers.'

'Sorry?'

'Well, even if they are a pain, even if they are miserable and controlling, I guess I do love my family, and I'm going to be going home once a year, hopefully with you, or we can drop you off somewhere and pick you up on the way back. Me and the baby, I mean. It might take a while to complete your gap year…' he grinned '…but you can do it in stages.'

And it was the nicest picture. It would be the first on her wall, one she would take to the shop tomorrow and have properly framed, because it wasn't the red dots, or the destinations, but the generosity that came with it—the acceptance, the space, the future they would create.

And she could do this, Alison realised.

She could love and she could live, and, yes, it might be scarier than safe, but it was nicer than safe, better than safe, and anyway Nick made her feel safe.

'Choose the honeymoon.'

'You don't have to marry me.'

'Actually, I do,' Nick said. 'Makes me feel more secure.' And then he grinned, and grinned even wider as a delicious thought struck. 'Oh, God,' said Nick, 'you know what this means…'

He was grinning and sounding delighted. 'No condoms. Monogamy, here I come.'

They had to undress in the dark because there were no curtains and would have to be up at the crack of dawn if they didn't want to be on public display.

'I don't like the look of this,' he warned as he pushed at the inflatable bed. 'I think it needs more air.'

'It's been filling for ages,' Alison said. 'You go first.' Because she'd rather topple onto him than have him topple onto her.

'It's comfortable.' Nick sounded surprised and he took her hand as she climbed in beside him and lay a moment adjusting to floating on air—her first night in her flat and Nick was beside her, and she lay there for a moment, trying to fathom how in so little time her life had changed, was changing, and would keep on doing so.

He rolled towards her and she lay in silence, could feel him watching.

'Are you happy, Alison?'

'I think…' She thought and paused as she examined her heart. 'That I'm going to have to get used to being happy.'

'Hey!' Nick said. 'We could move in with your mum, save a bit of money—rent this place out…' She kicked him, which wasn't a great idea in that bed because he almost fell out, and he held on like he was climbing up onto a life raft.

'It's a bit awkward,' Nick said, and he was right. It was awkward, less then two months in and suddenly here they were, except, she realised, Nick was talking about the bed, because he toppled onto her with a touch more gusto than intended, his lips meeting hers. They were warm and firm as she had so often remembered and his tongue was smooth and warm and tasted of Nick. And he was here, and that was going to take some getting used to, that this gorgeous, stunning man was here, not for baby, not for duty, but for her.

'I'm scared,' Nick said, and she was about to admit again that she was too—scared of telling everyone, scared of the future, scared that what they had found was too good to last—except as he came up for air, again Alison realised that he was talking about the bed. 'That we're going to topple over.'

There was the difference. Nick was in the now, living in the present, and for Alison grief and tragedy meant she lived with every scenario, every vision, knew how easily it all could change. And she wanted his faith and his presence in each moment, and she stepped into it as he moved deep within her, she let her mind still, concentrated on nothing more than the pleasure he gave her, focused on the now and all that they were.

And it was a precarious position, a shift to the left or the right and the passion that was building would crumble, but he locked his arms under her, cocooned her middle, trapped her where she wanted to be.

'I've got you.'

And she knew that he wasn't talking about the bed, that she was safe, and that they didn't need cartwheels. Just a dodgy bed and the other's body was enough for them.

EPILOGUE

'WHAT are you doing?'

Nick woke up and found her standing in the dark kitchen on tiptoe. 'Looking at our ocean view.' It was the only room in the house you could see it from. Right there between a couple of buildings there was their glimpse of the ocean, and even if it was tiny and she had to stand on tiptoe to see it, every day Alison did so, and tonight she had to see it too.

Her mum had been absolutely delighted, of course. She'd be delighted to babysit so that Alison could work, but only a couple of evenings if Alison was on a late shift, because Rose was busy getting her own life back.

And, of course, Nick's parents hadn't taken

it so well—this Australian hussy who had dragged their son screaming from his lovely structured life—but she and Nick had spent a couple of months in the UK and his parents had been over for a visit and were coming in three weeks when their grandchild was due.

'Come back to bed,' Nick said, because he'd worked the previous night and had been up all day, trying to turn what was surely a cupboard into a nursery. But more importantly he was loving this last trimester. Who would have thought pregnancy could be so sexy?

'My waters broke.' Just like that, Alison said it. 'Half an hour ago.'

'And you didn't wake me?'

'I just wanted…' Alison gave a little shrug '…a bit of time before everything happens.' And he heard the wobble in her voice and she was such a deep little thing, and he could see, even in the darkness, the sparkle of tears in her eyes, which meant she was scared. And though he never wanted her to be, he accepted that sometimes she was.

'You've got time,' he said, even when she bent over with a contraction. 'How far apart?'

'Ages,' Alison said.

'Come on,' Nick said, and he took her back to their bed, and he understood exactly where she was coming from because part of him didn't want the rest of the world right now, didn't want to ring the hospital or the excited, expectant families. He wanted just a little bit more time that was just for them.

And always he surprised her. Every morning, every night, every day he surprised her, because he was hers, because he got her, because he made her more of herself, and they surprised each other too.

Like this morning.

She had never trusted in them more completely, in him, in herself.

She had thought about labour, as to how it should be, would be, might be, and had prepared, she thought, for every eventuality, was open to drugs and epidurals and a Caesar if it had to be. She had scared herself senseless while never imagining this.

To lie in their bed, with him beside her, with no rush and no haste.

To be held and kissed for that first couple of hours, because that wasn't in any of the books, and they certainly weren't sexy kisses, just confirmation, and then later, just to be held and stroked as the pains deepened.

And then later, to be locked so deep in pain and know he was there at the other end, to close her eyes and go with it and to hear his lovely silence. She didn't want to move, didn't want to leave their little nest.

And he thought about it.

Dr Nick, who had been, till that moment, had anyone bothered to ask, against home births, for all the obvious reasons, found himself outside the obvious and so deep in the moment that, yes, he thought about breaking the rules and having his babe at home.

'We need to go to the hospital.' He was reluctantly practical. 'We really need to go now.' He climbed out of bed and wanted to climb back in, but he went and got the car out of the garage and rang the hospital, and helped her down the stairs.

She could feel the salty air on her lips and the cool of the morning, and she knew they'd left it a bit late, because the sun was peeking up and she was so, so ready to bear down.

The first bus of the morning was idling, passengers climbing in, and she hoped they all looked around to their fellow passengers and maybe met the person that bettered them, that every one of them could be as lucky as her.

'We're going to get told off,' Nick said as they pulled in at Maternity a little later.

'You'll get told off,' Alison said, really trying not to push. 'You're the doctor!'

But they didn't get told off, because everybody loved Nick.

And, yes, they'd spoken briefly about it once, but Alison had quickly declined. There was no way she'd let him deliver their baby, no way on earth, except the birthing suite was all dark and lovely, and if she closed her eyes she could almost be at home. The midwife was just glorious, just so calm and non-invasive, but Alison was glad she was there, and just very glad to hear Nick's voice.

'Come on, Alison, one more and the head will be out.'

It was the midwife holding her leg and Nick

holding their baby's head, and it had all happened so naturally, far, far nicer than she could ever have envisaged. And she pushed as hard as she could till he told her to stop and, yes, it hurt, but in a moment her baby was there and it was Nick who had delivered her.

Her, because he couldn't help himself from saying it.

'She's perfect.'

She was.

Blonde and long limbed and completely her father's daughter, because with one look Alison's heart was taken, and like it or not there could be no holding back—she already loved her.

'Some souvenir!' Nick smiled a little while later, when holding his daughter for the first time.

'More than you bargained for?' Alison asked, but Nick shook his head.

'More than I could ever have envisioned.' He tore his eyes away from his daughter and towards Alison. 'And I did.'

'And in these visions,' Alison checked, 'did your daughter have a name?'

'Martha.'

'Martha?' Alison went to shake her head, but stopped because, as she was starting to trust, this was his dream too.

Here was their biggest adventure.

* * * * *